BINGO, BRIBES, AND ALIBIS

A BREEZE VILLAGE COZY MYSTERY

KATE MACLEAN

BINGO, BRIBES, AND ALIBIS

CHAPTER 1

A sizzling speck of bacon grease jumped from the pan, landing on Virginia's forearm and yanking her from her daydream. She hissed and took a step back from the stove, but before she could react further, her son Jack stepped up behind her, easing her away from the hot surface and taking her place.

"I've got it," she grumbled but didn't fight him. Months of living with her son had reminded her how fruitless it was to argue with him. Jack knew best, and when he didn't, it usually wasn't worth it to push him on it. At least, that's what Virginia told herself as she retreated to the kitchen island and picked up her glass of milk.

Breakfast for dinner was her idea, the foolproof meal she thought she'd make for Jack and Stephanie to show her appreciation that they'd let her stay with them for so long. And now, like the lasagna the week before and the casserole the week before that, she found herself stepping back while Jack took over, trying not to let herself think about how dependent she'd become on her children.

"How was work today?" Stephanie asked, perched on an upholstered bar chair beside Virginia. Her dark brown hair was tied back in her usual ponytail, a slight flush to her face in the Southern summertime heat.

"It was fine," Virginia answered, trying to recall the shift just hours before. "Ronald came in today. He's doing well." She'd seen the man at Breeze Village when visiting Marney and usually challenged him to a game of poker when she had time, but it had been a few weeks since she'd been to visit. Marney had been increasingly busy preparing to open an online store selling her crocheted goods, and the more time passed while Virginia waited for her name to reach the top of the Breeze Village waitlist, the more frustration she felt visiting the place she was waiting to call home.

"Is it awkward when you see people you know at work?"

"No," Virginia said with a shrug. Eighty years old and one of the most social women in her small town, it would be more surprising if Virginia made it through a shift at the doctor's office *without* seeing someone she knew come through. "The awkward ones are the people I don't know who stare at me and then tell me they saw me in the paper."

The Seaview Gazette had run an article featuring Virginia and Dylan with the headline, "Seaview Senior Solves Murders," and once Virginia got over the picture they'd run alongside the article, she'd quite enjoyed the recognition. Now, months removed from the victory and battling the frustrations of living with her children and relinquishing her independence, the excitement of being recognized in the wild was replaced with something less joyful. People saw her as a hero, a victor, someone smart, someone who fought for those who couldn't fight for themselves, but the more time dragged on, Virginia saw herself as a burden, the parent becoming the child, dependent on the goodwill of her children for most everything.

Virginia's phone rang, the ringtone a full-volume imitation of the landline ringtone she missed so dearly, and all three of them started. Stephanie's hand flew to her chest, and she giggled at her reaction. Virginia could see Jack exhaling, stifling his anger, his default response to something surprising. Marney's name popped up on her phone's screen and Virginia's heart quickened. *My friend.*

Virginia snatched the phone up from the kitchen island and moved into the living room as she answered it. "Hello?"

"You have *got* to get over here," her friend gushed on the other end of the line.

"What's going on?" Even despite the lack of fear in Marney's voice, the urgency took Virginia back to the events of the spring, when her insistence on pursuing the investigation into the Breeze Village murders nearly got her friend killed. She breathed through the nausea that rose up in her throat as she remembered the sound of Marney's head hitting the concrete, passed out on the sidewalk while Matt aimed a gun at her.

"Nothing's the matter," Marney said quickly, sensing the panic in her friend's voice. "Michelle sold Breeze Village."

"What?"

"And the new owner is a *hunk!*" The smile on Marney's face shone through in her voice. "I'm telling you, you've got to get over here and meet him."

A smile crept over Virginia's face and the panic from moments earlier quieted. As she hung up the phone and turned back to the kitchen, she could see both Jack and Stephanie pointedly not listening, both suddenly very interested in their drinks.

"Breeze Village has a new owner," Virginia told them.

Jack lifted his eyebrows and curled his mouth into a perfect "O" shape, his faux surprised face utterly unconvincing. Stephanie smiled, but concern shone through her eyes. "Is that a good thing? Michelle warmed up to you after the whole… incident, right?"

Virginia grimaced involuntarily. She would never forget the shame she felt when Michelle had banned her from the Breeze Village premises earlier that year after she'd humiliated herself and injured Ronald. She'd been entirely convinced Haley, now her favorite nurse in the community, was going to poison his tea, and in her attempt to save his life she'd caused him massive burns on his legs.

"She has." Virginia nodded, shaking off the memory. "But it sounds like this new owner is a sight for sore eyes. Maybe he's the one I really want warming up to me." With a sly smile, she picked up her purse and shuffled to the shoe rack by the front door, sliding her sneakers onto her feet. "I'm going to go see for myself."

"You're not even going to wait until after dinner?" Jack

didn't conceal his annoyance as he moved the strips of bacon from the pan onto a paper towel-lined plate.

"You two keep asking me whether I know anything about the status of the waitlist, the timeline of my move. You clearly want me out of here. So I'd say it's important for me to make a good impression on this guy."

Stephanie stood up, guilt plastered on her face. "We're not trying to hurry you out of here. We know you're excited to finally make the move, and we're excited for you."

"Uh huh," Virginia said, kissing her daughter-in-law on the cheek. "Well, hopefully you can be excited for me and excited for yourselves soon. I'm off to go meet my new future landlord."

She reached up and fingered the silver pendant hanging from her neck, a Mother's Day gift from the kids. Though she was excited to see Marney and meet this new owner, she was nervous. She'd worked so hard to get back into Michelle's good graces, and now she'd be starting over with someone new.

With Jack and Stephanie both standing in the doorway watching her, she lifted her chin and made her way across the lawn to her car before she could second-guess herself.

TWENTY MINUTES LATER, Virginia was pulling into the parking lot of Breeze Village. Spanish moss dripped from towering live oaks framing the building. The light blue siding of the main building contrasted against the brilliant white of the shutters, door, and trim. Jane, as usual, sat in one of the rocking chairs on the large front porch. Her oxygen tank sat by her feet, and she rocked back and forth in the chair as she knit. She was the first person Virginia had seen when she first came to Breeze Village on the day Marney moved in. Then, Virginia had thought she looked a waif of a woman, just moments away from death. The sight of her had brought fear to Virginia's heart, a reminder of Marney's, and her own, age and the direction they were heading. Now, Virginia still thought Jane looked a waif of a woman inches from death, but she knew better.

"Virginia," Jane said, lifting her face and giving Virginia a smile. Her eyes shone with a fierce brilliance, hinting at the strength hiding within that frail frame draped with near-translucent skin. "It's been a while."

"Jane." Virginia returned the smile. "What are you knitting?"

"A sweater," Jane said, spreading the fuchsia fabric over her lap. "It's for Marney, but don't tell her. I figured if I started now, it might be ready by Christmas."

Virginia's throat tightened, and she thought back to the brunch when Marney had first told her she was moving into Breeze Village. She'd been so nervous to tell her best friend that she put it off until the day before the move, and then Virginia proved her right by lashing out in response. She'd been furious, hurt, and embarrassed, and she'd tried to convince her friend not to move here. Now, standing on the porch as the summer sun dipped toward the horizon, she felt shame flush her cheeks at the idea that she would have kept her friend from the love and friendships she'd found here.

"It's lovely."

Inside the main building, the lobby was bustling. The familiar scent washed over Virginia, and what she'd once found too sterile now felt comforting.

"There you are!" Marney rushed from the dining room into the lobby, where Virginia was signing in at the front desk, and wrapped her in a hug. "I was worried you wouldn't come."

"Well, I wouldn't want to miss my chance to meet the hunky new owner, would I?" Virginia said with a grin.

Marney grinned back and tipped her head toward the small office off the lobby, which adjoined the nurses' station. "They're in there." Virginia looked toward the cracked door. Inside, she could see Michelle's gray-blond bob bouncing as she spoke, her back to the door. Virginia couldn't hear what was being said, but she could see that the ancient computer atop the large wooden desk had been replaced by a sleeker model and the towering filing cabinets that had lined the walls of the office were nearly all gone. Several new bookshelves filled the space the cabinets left behind.

"When did she sell?" Virginia asked. "It seems like they've already made a lot of changes."

Marney shrugged. "There have been a few new people hired recently, and they've been moving things around in there, but Michelle didn't mention the sale until today. This is the first any of us have seen of Russ."

"Russ," Virginia repeated, weighing the name on her tongue, putting it alongside the figure she could see behind Michelle. He was tall and muscular, with hair the color of espresso, and he wore a bored expression on his face. Virginia found herself staring, wishing Michelle would take a step to the side and reveal the rest of his figure, when he suddenly held up a hand to Michelle and stepped around her.

"Can I help you?" His dark eyes bore down on Virginia and she felt rooted to the spot, stomach sinking. Every word in her lexicon vanished from her brain.

"This is Virginia," Marney said, wrapping her arm around one of Virginia's and pulling her in close. "And I'm Marney."

"Virginia," Michelle said coolly, stepping out of the office and joining them in the lobby, "solved the murders that occurred here earlier this spring. And Marney is one of our residents. She lives in one of the cottages out back."

Russ said nothing, just looking them up and down. Virginia squirmed under his gaze. Marney stood tall beside her.

"Virginia's on the waitlist," Marney added, "so soon she'll be a resident here, too." She beamed up at Russ, not flinching away from his discerning gaze or tight frown.

"Yes, well, we'll be making some changes, of course. Including changes to the waitlist." Russ's voice was low, and Virginia had to strain to hear.

"What sorts of changes?" Virginia asked.

"That remains to be decided." Russ turned away from them as if bored with the conversation. "Likely changes to the eligibility requirements, possibly eliminating it altogether."

Virginia couldn't form a thought, couldn't string

together the words to respond. As Russ walked away, dress shoes clicking on the tile floor, the room seemed to spin around her. Michelle followed Russ back into the office and closed the door behind them, leaving Virginia and Marney standing arm-in-arm in the center of the lobby.

"Did he say they're eliminating the waitlist?" Virginia choked out.

Marney wrapped her in a hug. "It'll be all right."

Virginia frowned and pushed away from her friend. "But he did say that, right?" When Marney began to repeat herself, Virginia interrupted her. "I'm not asking about whether it'll be fine. I'm asking if I heard him correctly."

"I think so," Marney said quietly.

"Can they even do that?" Confusion turned to anger, and as Virginia raised her voice she felt eyes on her and was suddenly aware of the full dining room attached to the lobby, all heads turned toward them. When Virginia looked in their direction, some of the residents turned back to their plates, but several looked on, waiting for the dinner show to continue.

"Let's go to my cottage," Marney said, giving Virginia's arm a gentle tug. There was pleading in her eyes. *Please don't make a scene,* they seemed to say. *Please don't embarrass me.*

Cheeks flushed, Virginia looked down at her sneakers and let Marney lead her through the dining room and out the French doors that led to the courtyard. The sun had nearly completed its sinking beneath the horizon, a blaze of orange piercing the deep purple. Virginia forced herself to lift her head, to take it in, to exhale.

"Can they do this?" she asked again, voice quieter.

Marney squeezed her hand and resumed walking, leading them through the courtyard and to the row of cottages at the back of the property.

Inside Marney's cottage, the small gray tabby cat Virginia had taken from Matt's and Christine's property lounged on Marney's red-checkered loveseat. The little guy had completely made himself at home here in the last few months, gladly trading the freedom of the great outdoors for the comforts of indoor living. A small fountain bubbled in the corner of the room next to a bowl of kibble, and Marney had left the television on in the background. The sounds of a home renovation series filled the space.

"It's going to be fine," Marney said, cutting Virginia off the moment she'd opened her mouth.

"I just don't think it's right," Virginia countered, the shame at making a scene fading back into anger.

"We don't even know what changes they're going to make. Can we wait for them to definitively tell you they're taking you off the waitlist before we freak out?"

Virginia opened her mouth to argue but saw the desperation in her friend's face. Marney had avoided confrontation the entire time Virginia had known her. Life with an abusive husband had taken its toll. But since her life was entirely upheaved in the spring, Marney had seemed quicker to shrink into her shell than before. The slightest conflict sent her spiraling into panic attacks. Even a spirited round of cards could set her off. Virginia and Ronald had gotten into it after a game a month before when Marney had quietly gotten up and made her way out of the dining room and back to her cottage. She hadn't said anything, but Virginia could see the trembling as Marney hurried away and felt guilty for causing her distress.

"Fine," Virginia said, softening. She reached out and took Marney's hand in her own, squeezing it gently. "I'm going to go see Gemma. I haven't seen her since she moved in last week."

Her friend and the president of the Garden Review Society had moved into another one of Breeze Village's independent living cottages the week before, only two doors down from Marney, and Virginia was anxious to see how she was settling in. She was also anxious to vent to someone she knew would appreciate it. With a quick kiss on Marney's cheek and another on Pancake's head, she made her way back into the humid evening air and over to the cottage Gemma now occupied.

THOUGH SHE'D ONLY JUST MOVED in, Gemma had already made her cottage her own. A bright sunflower flag hung from a small iron pole stuck into the ground beside her front porch, and tiered plant stands held dahlias in various shades of peach, pink, and purple, framing both sides of the front door. A cheeky doormat peered up at Virginia from beneath her feet. *COME BACK WHEN YOU HAVE WINE.* The door was cracked, letting the breeze drift into the small space, and music spilled from within.

"Knock knock," Virginia said as she pushed open the door and poked her head in. "You've got a visitor!"

Gemma squealed with delight, rushing from her small kitchen to the door to wrap her friend in a hug. Her hands were coated in some doughy substance so she held them high and let Virginia embrace her instead.

"Are you baking?" In the decades Virginia had known Gemma, she'd never known her to bake. She was terrible in the kitchen. Her primary motivation for moving into Breeze Village was not having to cook for herself anymore.

"They say it's important to take up new hobbies in retirement," Gemma said with a shrug. She returned to the kitchen and Virginia followed her, helping herself to a glass of water and leaning against the countertop while she watched her friend plunge her hands back into a bowl of sticky dough.

"What are you making?"

"Naan bread. Do you want to help?"

"Why not? I'm sure you could use it." Virginia chuckled and downed the rest of her water before scooting in close to Gemma and leaning over to inspect the dough. "Is it supposed to be so… goopy? And lumpy?"

Gemma threw her head back in a laugh. "You don't beat around the bush, do you? Honestly, I have no clue what it's supposed to be like. The recipe said it would be wet and sticky, and I think I've achieved that."

"Oh, you definitely have."

Gemma dug her hands into the bowl again, attempting to knead the dough but having little success due to the fact that the dough was the consistency of a runny cake batter. Her dark skin contrasted with the light dough, and both stood in contrast to the brilliant color everywhere else in the space. "I'm supposed to roll this into six balls," Gemma said, lifting a hand from the bowl and watching the mixture drip from her fingers.

"Maybe more flour?" Virginia suggested, stepping in to do what she could to save the bake. She wasn't a whiz in the kitchen, but she enjoyed it. Especially in the company of someone whose first inclination as things went up in smoke was to toss her head back and laugh.

"I have a confession," Virginia began once the dough was beginning to take shape. "I didn't come just to check in on you. Well, I did want to see how you're getting along now that you've moved in, but I also wanted to talk with you about something. Something I can't talk with Marney about."

"Sugar, I know you came looking for me because you needed me. And it turns out I needed you," she said with a gesture toward the six balls Virginia was rolling out on parchment paper. "So, spit it out! What's going on?"

"The new owner, Russ—have you met him?"

In reply, Gemma merely let out a low whistle.

"That's what I thought, too. I was so ready to like him, so ready to come gossip with you over the way his muscles ripple out from his rolled-up sleeves—"

Gemma cut her off with a groan of agreement.

"But when Marney told him I'm on the waitlist, he said they're making changes to it and might eliminate it altogether. I might not be able to move into Breeze Village." She'd barely let herself think those words, and voicing them brought up the tears she'd quelled until then.

"Oh, honey." Gemma took her in her arms, no longer worried about her messy hands, and held Virginia while she took big gulps of air and tried to stop crying. When the tears had stopped, Gemma released her from the hug and stood back, hands on Virginia's shoulders. "Virginia Walker, you are one of the strongest, most headstrong people I have ever had the pleasure of knowing. You are not a woman who lets people walk all over her. Are you going to let this man make decisions for your life?"

The tears threatened to spring forward again at the compliment. Virginia opened her mouth to tell Gemma that's not how it works, that Russ owned Breeze Village now and it was his prerogative to make these decisions, but Gemma held up a hand and stopped her.

"You solved the murders of three residents of this retirement community this year. It is because of you that those families have closure, that this community has closure. You will not let this man tell you that you can't have your rightful place here with the rest of us. Now," she said, stepping back with her hands on her hips, "I want you to walk back in there and remind this Russ fellow of who you are and where you belong. You belong here, and he is not going to keep that from you."

By the end of Gemma's speech, Virginia felt a spark kindling in her stomach. *I belong here, and no one is going to keep that from me.*

She stepped forward, wrapping Gemma in another embrace. "Thank you," she whispered.

As Virginia walked back toward the door, she called over her shoulder, "Don't forget to grease that pan. And the place looks great, by the way." She took in the space Gemma had filled with color—a brilliant green velvet couch, a bright yellow TV stand, a magenta lampshade with multicolored fringe hanging from it, and art on every wall—and bid her friend goodbye. Then she made her way across the courtyard, breathing deeply and trying to stoke that newly burning fire inside her for the looming confrontation.

THE DINING ROOM wasn't empty when Virginia reentered through those beautiful French doors, but it was considerably less full than it had been before. A few people still sat eating their dinners, and several tables had taken up card games or lively conversation. Virginia ignored the dip in volume as she strode across the room, tried to make her steps smooth, make herself appear strong and put together. She could feel the eyes on her, but she didn't meet them, keeping her own eyes focused on the door off the lobby leading to Russ's office.

She stood in front of the heavy wooden door, breathing in for six counts before releasing it, one of the many calming techniques Marney's therapist had taught her in the past few months. Finally, she lifted a fist to knock when the door swung open. Virginia gasped, suddenly greeted by Russ's dominating figure in the doorway.

"Virginia." His voice was low and smooth, like he wasn't surprised at all to see her there. His gaze assessed her once more, and she couldn't help but squirm beneath it, lowering her eyes to her feet. "How may I help you?"

Another deep breath. In, two, three, four, five, six. Then out.

Virginia returned her gaze to Russ's face, steeling herself. "I wanted to talk with you about the waitlist." She thought she saw a hint of amusement dance in Russ's eyes. A twinkle of surprise that Virginia had come to confront him rather than roll over and take what he offered.

"Please, come in." Russ stepped back into the small office, beckoning for Virginia to follow him. Russ took a seat in a sleek chair behind the hulking desk and gestured toward the chair opposite him. Rather than sit, Virginia stood behind the chair, gripping its back. She waited for Russ to speak further, but he just looked up at her expectantly.

"I wanted to talk with you about the waitlist," she repeated.

"Yes, you said as much." He rested his elbows on the dark wood of the desk, lacing his fingers and resting his chin on them. Gold rings glittered on three of his fingers, the largest of the three rings adorning his pinkie finger, which ended abruptly at the first digit. Virginia wondered how he'd lost it.

You belong here.

"I solved three murders here earlier this year." Pride rose in her as she voiced her accomplishment. "In doing so, I spent quite a bit of time here. This community became my own. Without me, no one would have looked into Ruth Beaumont's death, and she never would have gotten justice."

She waited for Russ's response. He only continued to stare up at her.

"I've been on this waitlist for months. I know this is a

highly desirable place to live, and I would never ask to jump ahead in line or anything like that. But I do want the place here that I was promised. When a room opens up, and it's my turn, I should be allowed to move in here as planned."

Russ nodded almost imperceptibly, his mouth drawn thin. Virginia held her ground, willing herself to meet his gaze despite the pounding in her chest.

"An understandable request," Russ finally said. "But you must understand, I've just come to own this retirement home, and I have to think about the business. It would be… irresponsible of me to let things continue that don't serve the business's best interests."

Virginia narrowed her brows in confusion.

"Money." Russ's abrupt statement caught Virginia off guard. "The waitlist is full of people who will need payment plans, or to whom Michelle promised a discount or any number of things that are not in line with how I intend to run this place."

Virginia took a step forward, gripping the chair in front of her tighter as she tried to make sense of what Russ was telling her. "You're kicking me off the waitlist to make more money? I wasn't promised a discount, and I won't be on a payment plan."

Russ shrugged. "Dissolving the waitlist and implementing a new system with clearer terms is the way I want to go, and I am the one in charge now. Although, if I thought it was in the business's best interest to make sure you got what you wanted…" Russ's gaze held Virginia's as he trailed off. "If I knew that your moving into Breeze

Village would be, let's say, advantageous to the business, then I might reconsider."

"What are you saying?"

"It's expensive to run this place. If there were some… incentive… for me to keep Michelle's promise to you and let you move in, then I would have to consider it."

Virginia felt her mouth drop open and promptly closed it in an attempt to maintain her composure. "A bribe?"

Russ leaned back, holding his hands up in front of him. "I never said that."

"You as good as did." Virginia felt heat flushing her face as her voice rose. "How dare you? You vile, arrogant, greedy bastard."

"Now, now, there's no need to get overly emotional."

At that, Virginia exploded. "Do not tell me what to feel when you've tried to bribe me in exchange for what is supposed to be my *home*." She jabbed a finger in Russ's direction, spittle flying from her lips as she yelled, crazed. "You are going to regret this decision. I will make sure of it."

Russ's calm demeanor as she laid into him enraged Virginia even further, and she spun on her heels, nearly throwing herself off balance as she lunged for the door and slammed it behind her. And there, in front of her, stood her friend Ronald with two of Russ's new staff hires. Ronald was grinning from ear to ear, showing off his few remaining teeth. The two staff members looked stunned.

Embarrassment rose in Virginia as the two of them murmured to each other and avoided her gaze. Ronald gave her a clap on the back before hobbling toward the elevator, laughing to himself. "Crazy old cook," she thought she heard him say.

Virginia hurried out the door, down the wooden steps, and over to her car before letting the tears flow.

CHAPTER 2

Jack and Stephanie were on the couch watching a movie when Virginia returned home. *Jack's home. Stephanie's home. Not my home. My home doesn't exist anymore.*

They turned as she shut the door behind her and hung her purse from one of the hooks hanging on the entryway wall. Each of them had narrowed eyes—Jack's a keen, assessing gaze, and Stephanie's concerned and pitying. Virginia wondered how she must look to elicit those looks from her children.

"What happened?" Jack asked, already on his feet and crossing the room. He took one of Virginia's hands in his own, his other arm wrapping around her shoulders so he could lead her to the couch where Stephanie remained.

Virginia shrugged him off. "The new owner is a prick. I'm going to bed."

"Whoa, whoa, whoa, what happened?" Stephanie stood and approached Virginia.

"He's getting rid of the waitlist so he can pick and

choose who to let into Breeze Village and only take the ones that'll make him the most money. He all but said I could pay him a bribe to keep my spot and be allowed to move in."

Stephanie's eyes were wide. She looked surprised and disgusted. Jack already had his phone in hand and was scrolling through his contacts.

"Stop," Virginia told him. "Don't try to fix this for me. Not yet, at least. I want to figure this out myself."

"If we had a contract," Jack said, ignoring his mother, "it was with Breeze Village, not Michelle. It doesn't matter who owns the place." He held the phone up to his ear but kept talking. "This guy sounds like a real piece of work. Do we really want you living there now that it's under his ownership? What about Harbor Vale?"

Stephanie nodded, eager to latch onto a solution and diffuse the situation. "Or there are some cute duplexes not even ten minutes down the road. A friend of mine just got in-home care for her father, and they've been really happy."

Jack's attention had turned to his phone call, apparently to his sister. "Lucy, Mom just got home talking about the new Breeze Village owner. We might need to figure out alternative living arrangements."

All around her, the conversation flowed as if Virginia weren't present, as if she were a problem to be solved, not the one to solve the problems. After the evening she'd had, it was too much.

"I said *stop*." She took the phone from Jack's hand, and his eyes went wide with shock. "Lucy," she said into the receiver, "everything is fine. Goodnight." After hanging up the phone, she turned back to her son and his wife, who were both staring at her in disbelief. "Now, I'm going to go to bed. You're going to finish watching your movie. You're going to let me figure this out myself, and you will not step in and offer me help unless I ask for it."

Jack narrowed his eyes, his mouth drawn taut. Stephanie nodded and choked out an apology. Virginia turned and walked down the hall to her room—*not my room, the guest room*—and gripped the dresser with both hands, feeling like she might fall over.

As she dressed for bed, she found herself looking at her phone, expecting Marney's or Lawrence's name to pop up on the screen. Her chest ached as she willed her friends to reach out to her. By the time she'd brushed her teeth, slathered lotion over her face and neck, donned a satin bonnet, and crawled in between the sheets, she'd given up on them and moved on to contemplating her options.

The thought of handing over money to Russ made her stomach churn. The realization that the money would have to be her children's, as she had very little of it to her name, intensified the nausea. She was excited to move into Breeze Village because the community had become a home to her, or as close as she thought anyplace besides the house Bellemeade had leveled could be. Moving into Harbor Vale or some duplex or apartment away from Marney, away from her friends, felt unimaginable. The sounds of the television filtered down the hallway and into Virginia's room, and she fell into a fitful sleep.

* * *

THE SUMMER SUN beat down on the large white tent outside the American Legion, where Virginia sat across from Lawrence at one of a dozen wooden picnic tables. She peered over at the card in front of him and scowled. It was a bingo tournament to raise money for his bowling league, and Lawrence was kicking her butt.

"N39," the leader called out, and Virginia smacked her pen down in frustration.

Lawrence chuckled as he filled in yet another square on his card.

"Aren't you supposed to be looking for love here, anyway? Not kicking my ass in bingo?"

Lawrence had recently decided, inspired by seeing Marney open up for the first time since leaving Dean, that he, too, was ready to face love again after loss. Virginia had never expected him to want to date again. Losing Ben had changed Lawrence in a way she understood, in a way she knew one never fully recovered from. When Lawrence came to her, palms sweating, eyes darting around, and choked out the words to ask her to help him get back out there, she'd thought she'd gone crazy. But then he'd repeated himself, said he was serious, and Virginia marveled as her brave friend put himself out there, opening himself up to more pain in the name of filling this chapter of life with more love.

Lawrence grinned up at her, but behind his coffee brown eyes, Virginia swore she saw something like nerves. "I can look for love and kick your ass at the same time. Besides, I already know everyone here, and none of them are 'potential next love' material."

"What about potential next roll in the sheets material?"

Virginia looked around at the bingo crowd. At eighty, she and Lawrence were right around the middle of the pack in age. Lawrence was far and away the most attractive person there, but she spied another man two tables over who looked in remarkable shape for his age. "What about that guy? I don't know that guy. You know that guy?"

"I know that guy," Lawrence mumbled, lowering his gaze. "Don't point!"

Virginia let out a low whistle. "Oh, you *know* that guy!"

"Bingo!" someone shouted, and Lawrence jumped up to get new cards for himself and Virginia.

When he returned, he looked less than amused. "His name is Arthur. I went on a few dates with him. It didn't work out, and I'm not answering any more questions about it."

"Fine," Virginia acquiesced. "I guess as your wing-woman, I don't need to know your entire dating history, although I maintain that context is helpful. And fun."

They played in silence for a while, Virginia's card filling more quickly this time around. With every spot she filled in, she felt the anticipation of an impending triumph. When someone at the next table got bingo before she did, she felt the childish urge to toss her nearly-complete card on the ground in frustration and jealousy.

"Easy now," Lawrence said, seeing Virginia danger-ously close to boiling over. "Marney said you guys met the new Breeze Village owner yesterday evening. It didn't sound like it went especially well."

Distracted from her loss, Virginia frowned. "He's

awful, Lawrence. Awful. Just a real jerk, and…" She struggled to get the rest out. "And he's planning on getting rid of the waitlist."

Concern spread across Lawrence's handsome face. "What do you mean, get rid of the waitlist?"

"Kick me and everyone else off and only let people into Breeze Village who are prepared to pay out the wazoo. The asshole implied that I could bribe him so he'd let me move in as planned."

Lawrence almost smiled, and Virginia kicked him under the table. "What's that for?"

"I'm just impressed you're sitting here, telling me this story, ostensibly going over your options before making a move. I think a previous Virginia might have just run off to a casino, determined to fix this herself without even letting the people who love her the most know what situation she was in."

A wave of pride swelled in Virginia, along with a wave of curiosity. "Vegas is pretty far, even for my pig-headed self."

"Fortune Star Casino is only a few hours away, on the Cherokee reservation." When Lawrence saw Virginia's intrigue, his smile fell. "No," he said sternly. "Don't even think about it."

"I'm not," Virginia insisted, even as she dug in her pocketbook and pulled out her phone. She opened up a browser and searched for the casino, pulling up its website. Sure enough, not even three hours away, there was a casino with poker tables and slot machines and endless potential to flush money down the drain. And there, at the top of the screen, was a big blue banner. In block letters, it read *BINGO TOURNAMENT JUNE 3-5.*

"No," Lawrence repeated, reading over Virginia's shoulder. "It's a bad idea."

Virginia hardly heard him. She was too busy looking at all the zeros of the grand prize. Her wheels spun as she considered the entry cost, the travel, and arrangements for accommodations. It was a lot, she decided. Too much. Unless...

"What if Breeze Village went as a group?" The idea sounded ridiculous even as it rolled off her lips, but she'd heard of Harbor Vale taking its residents on field trips. If Breeze Village took them, she wouldn't have to make the drive herself, and she'd have Marney there to keep her head on straight.

Lawrence made to disagree but was interrupted by Virginia's phone alarm. "I've got to go to work," she said, planting both hands on the wooden table and pushing herself up to stand. Her legs wobbled under her as she stepped over the bench, freeing herself from the picnic table.

"I don't think it's a good idea," Lawrence said in one final attempt to talk sense into her. "But I love you, and I hope your shift goes well."

He kissed her on the cheek, and Virginia was off to spend the remainder of the afternoon behind the desk at Dr. DiMarco's office. A few hours of scheduling patients, pulling files, and sorting all the files the doctor had pulled and then inevitably left scattered around. While she worked, she could think of nothing but the bingo tournament and the money to be won. Money that could buy her a spot in Breeze Village, the home she'd come to be so excited about.

She pictured handing the money over to Russ, a thick envelope passing from her hand to his, his smile as he took it making her stomach roil. *Dirty. If I do this, I'm stooping to his level.* But if she didn't do it, she risked losing her home. And the disgust and despair at losing yet another home overcame the disgust she felt at paying off a prick like Russ.

CHAPTER 3

Ten days after suggesting it to Liam, who she'd been informed by Gemma was Russ's right-hand man and the director of wellness programs or something like that, Virginia found herself on a tour bus with nearly a dozen Breeze Village residents. And only a few hours after that, she found herself stepping through the sliding glass doors of what didn't look too different from a regular hotel. The main difference was the addition of a flashing neon sign in the parking lot that advertised the casino attached to the hotel.

Gemma and Ronald hustled past her, Gemma eager to find the bar and Ronald eager to find the poker tables. Marney gripped Virginia's hand, squeezing it tightly as they followed Liam to their rooms. In her other hand, she clutched a frayed tote bag overflowing with yarn and crochet works in progress.

At dinner that evening, the group sipped sweet tea and traded trash talk, speculating on who would win big.

Virginia plastered a smile on her face and traded barbs with Ronald, but her heart wasn't in it. Instead, it thrummed in her ears as she pictured winning big. What it would buy her. What was at stake if she didn't.

"I'm going to bed," Marney said, yanking Virginia's attention back to the dining room. "Are you going to play a few rounds?"

A yawn escaped Virginia before she could reply. "At least a couple," she said, fighting the exhaustion. There was too much on the line to pass on the evening's games.

When Virginia returned to the room she and Marney shared almost two hours later, she expected to find Marney tucked into one of the beds, fast asleep. Instead, she found her sitting propped up against a mountain of pillows, a sweater rapidly taking formation in her hands.

"You don't have to sneak," Marney said by way of greeting.

"I didn't expect you to be up."

"Couldn't sleep."

Virginia turned to hide her wince. She knew why Marney now had trouble sleeping. Why she had weekly therapy appointments and two new medications in her daily routine.

It was because of Virginia. Because she'd dragged Marney into an investigation that turned dangerous. Because she'd put her best friend in harm's way.

"Don't start feeling guilty," Marney said as if she could read Virginia's thoughts. "I accidentally ordered a regular latte when we stopped for coffee earlier instead of a decaf."

As Virginia sat on the edge of the bed, slipping off her shoes and then her capris, coaxing her stiff fingers to grasp and undo the buttons of her shirt, she thought she didn't deserve Marney. Didn't deserve the forgiveness and compassion her friend extended to her time and time again. She bit her tongue to fight back tears.

If her first bingo games of the weekend had gone better, she might have had an easier time convincing herself that what Marney said was true. Instead, they'd gone poorly, and she was starting the weekend off in the red, out the entry fee and with nothing to show for it yet.

At breakfast the next morning, Virginia tried to tune out Gemma's excited boasting about already having won some money the night before. She sipped her coffee, trying to turn her attention to her breathing like Stephanie had taught her, like she saw Marney doing frequently now when she started to spiral into her anxiety.

"Mornin'!" Ronald slid into the chair next to hers, knocking the table and jostling Virginia's coffee from its cup.

She winced and forced what she hoped was more smile than grimace as she mopped up the mess with her napkin.

Ronald was unfazed. "Ready to win some big bucks?"

"Let's hope so."

As Virginia was finishing her toast, Marney drifted into the room. As usual, she'd brought her crochet with her. Before she could start in on her own breakfast, her phone dinged, and she lit up.

"Look what Jane sent me." Marney passed her phone to Virginia to show her the pictures of Pancake that Jane had sent. In the first picture, he lounged across the arm of Marney's sofa, luxuriating like a king. In the second picture, he was hanging from the drapes.

Virginia opened her mouth to respond, but a blood-curdling shriek cut through the room before she could say anything.

The scream echoed through the space. Virginia looked around along with the rest of the dining room crowd, trying to place where it came from. After the scream came silence, more frightening than the shriek itself, followed by a wailing like Virginia had never heard. It was an animal cry, all terror and heartbreak.

Liam leapt from where he'd been sitting and sipping coffee. His face was ghost white as he hurried from the dining room and toward the hall where the sound was coming from. It was the hall where their group was staying.

Another wail ripped through the space. Marney gasped, and Virginia realized she'd grabbed her friend's hand and was squeezing it. She dropped it with a whispered apology.

The seconds felt like hours as the entire room waited in silence. What might have been two minutes or twenty passed, and Liam returned to the dining room, this time with a sobbing woman draped over one shoulder, his arm around her lower back as he led her to a chair before kneeling beside her to comfort her. Virginia recognized the woman as Kim, the other of Russ's new hires she'd seen outside his office after their confrontation. Her ruby red hair hung in front of her face, sticking to her tear-soaked cheeks. Liam pressed a Styrofoam cup into her hand, but she was shaking too violently to drink the liquid it contained. Instead, it sloshed over her scrubs as she sobbed.

Liam's attempts to comfort Kim were utterly unsuccessful. Sirens began to wail in the distance, growing ever closer, and Kim continued to wail, rocking back and forth in her chair, clutching her arms around herself, and talking incoherently.

As she cried, Virginia thought she made out a couple words: "Russ" and "dead."

* * *

POLICE ARRIVED ON THE SCENE. They went first to Kim, then a group of them turned toward the hallway where she pointed them toward Russ's room. One officer remained with Kim, talking with her, comforting her, and, Virginia was sure, trying to get as much information from her as possible. As incoherent as she was, Virginia wondered whether any of it would be useful.

Another detective remained in the dining room, making his way from table to table, talking with everyone present.

"I wonder if the bastard had a heart attack," Gemma muttered. "Then again, he'd have to have a heart for that, I guess." She glanced at her watch and declared that they were going to be late for the start of day two of the tournament, but before she could exit the dining room, the detective stopped her.

"I'm going to need you all to remain where you are, please," he announced, giving Gemma an extra glance that said *don't try me.*

At the next table over, Virginia could hear two new residents speculating on what this meant for Breeze Village. One was a lively man, Dick, who used a cane or walker to get around but oozed enthusiasm all the same. The other was a large woman who Virginia had heard referred to as Patricia. Though she towered over Dick, Virginia wasn't sure she'd ever heard the woman speak. With her quiet demeanor, she managed to make herself invisible despite her physical presence.

"If I'd have moved into Harbor Vale instead of listening to my son, I wouldn't be dealing with all this chaos. Do you know how much stress increases the risk of a heart attack?"

Patricia nodded, lips pulled together tightly, while Dick ranted.

"I wonder if this means Michelle gets it back? Maybe we'll have the original Breeze Village experience after all," Dick continued. Michelle. She was back at Breeze Village, running the place while Russ had accompanied the group on their field trip. Virginia wondered if the news had reached her and the rest of the community yet.

One of the officers who had gone to Russ's room returned to the dining room and beckoned the detective over. The room fell silent while the two whispered. The detective frowned and turned back to the half-full room, passing his scrutinizing gaze over the diners. Virginia felt his gaze linger on her just a second longer than it did on anyone else, but then he turned away and she convinced herself she'd imagined it.

The first officer left, returning down the hall, and the detective resumed his rounds.

"Do you think something's happened?" Marney asked. "This seems like a lot of police for a heart attack."

Virginia's stomach sank.

"You mean like a murder?" Colleen asked. The psychic had been quiet the entire trip so far. Since Gemma had moved into Breeze Village, the two had become close, nearly joined at the hip, but on the drive up the day before, Colleen had hardly even spoken to Gemma. She'd gone straight to her room once they arrived.

Marney's face paled. She gave the slightest nod, and Virginia felt her own face pale at the thought. Another murder. Death seemed to be following Breeze Village. Following her.

"I'm sure it wasn't," Virginia said, sitting up a little straighter.

Just then, the detective approached their table. "I'd like to speak to each of you alone, if that's okay." The women all nodded. "You first." He gestured roughly toward Gemma, who followed him to an empty table a few yards away.

Virginia strained to hear what the detective asked, what Gemma answered. Marney and Colleen both looked down at their plates, pushing pieces of fruit around, occasionally sipping from their mugs of coffee and tea. At the next table over, Dick, Patricia, and Ronald talked in hushed tones.

Liam was still comforting Kim, whose sobs had quieted but who still looked disoriented and anguished. If Kim had found him, and if it was indeed something more serious than a heart attack, Virginia knew what Kim was feeling, and though she'd never had a conversation with the nurse, she wished she could go over and put her arm around her. Instead, she found Marney's hand with her own and gave it a gentle squeeze. She knew Marney was likely thinking the same thing, revisiting the night when they'd found a body in the hallway, lying in his own blood. The body of a man Marney was opening herself up to, a man she thought she could love.

Gemma returned to the table and looked to Virginia. "You're up."

"Are you Virginia Walker?"

Virginia's brows furrowed at the detective's direct question. "I am."

"Do you have a golden nail file with the initials VW on it?"

Dread built upon the confusion in Virginia's gut. She nodded but couldn't choke out a response.

"Can you tell me where it is?"

Virginia stammered, "It's in my purse." But when she opened her bag and dug through the contents, the nail file was gone.

"I don't understand," she said. Her hand shook as she dug with increasing fervor through her purse. "I had it. I was using it last night, after dinner…" She trailed off, trying to think of where she might have left it, but could come up with nothing.

"Can you tell me more about last night? Where you were, who you were with?"

"I don't understand," Virginia repeated. "What is this about?"

"Russ Farrell was murdered last night." Virginia sucked in a shallow breath. "And it seems your nail file was the murder weapon."

"My nail file? *My* nail file? My *nail file?*" Virginia repeated the words, shifting the emphasis every which way as she grew more incredulous each time. When the detective had announced that everyone was free to go, Marney had practically run back to their room, shuffling between the tables with more agility than Virginia knew she had in her. Virginia hurried after her with considerably less ease. She reached their room just as the door slammed shut in her face. She knocked, but Marney didn't open the door for her, and when she reached into her bag for her key, it wasn't there.

By the time she'd returned to the dining room to locate her forgotten room key and worked the door open, Marney was sitting propped on the bed, fingers flying as she worked her magic on yarn.

"What the heck, Marney?"

"Virginia, I just—" Marney stopped and took a deep breath before resuming in a lower voice. "I just need some quiet."

"My nail file was used to kill a man, and you need some quiet?"

"I can't handle thinking about it right now."

But it was all Virginia could think about. A few short months of peace, of victory, had come to a screeching halt with the sale of Breeze Village and the loss of the security that came with knowing where she'd be living by the end of the summer. And now any remaining semblance of peace was shattered by Kim's scream tearing through the high ceilings of the dining room, by Virginia's own nail file stabbed into the asshole who'd been so determined to take away her home. And it looked like she'd done it.

"Who would have wanted to frame me?" Virginia couldn't help it. She couldn't stop herself from speculating aloud as her mind reeled. "Why would they have taken my nail file?"

"Virginia, I don't know." The sharpness of Marney's voice stung, and Virginia finally quieted. Marney's face softened at her friend's reaction. "Maybe Colleen can help? Maybe she's had some sort of vision or something?"

Fat chance she'll be any help, Virginia thought. "She's been weirdly quiet lately. Withdrawn." But her friend, instead of just snapping at her, had offered her a suggestion. "I'll go talk to her."

A backward glance as she left their room revealed Marney's exasperated face crumpling. She looked so small against the pile of pillows, and Virginia turned away before she could confirm whether she'd seen a tear rolling down Marney's pale cheek.

The dining room was empty when Virginia stepped from the carpeted hallway into the large open space, her sneakers squeaking on the tile. A rectangular table off to one wall was draped in a navy tablecloth and contained the remnants of breakfast: a few picked-over pastries and an empty coffee urn. Virginia squeaked her way across the room, turning into the main atrium which led to the casino.

The event hall was off to her right, directly across from the glass doors leading out to the parking lot. If she continued straight ahead she'd enter the main casino floor, where she expected she'd find Ronald playing poker. Instead, she pulled open the door to the event hall, a half ballroom filled with seniors playing bingo, and looked around. Dick and Patricia sat together on the far side of the room, and Gemma was at the next table over. No Colleen.

Virginia slid into the empty chair next to Gemma. Gemma hardly seemed to notice. A wiry man on a podium at the front of the room spoke into a microphone. "G49."

"Bingo!" Gemma stood, her body pushing the table forward and sloshing the water glasses atop it as she raised her card triumphantly into the air.

By the time Gemma's card was approved and she made her way back out into the atrium with Virginia, she was glowing. It was her second victory so far, and Virginia worked to tamp down her jealousy. Her briber was dead, she reminded herself, taking a deep breath. She could relax.

"Have you seen Colleen?" Virginia asked. "I wanted to talk to her about, well, about Russ."

A wicked grin spread across Gemma's face. "I heard

about the murder weapon." She lowered her voice. "Did you do it? I won't tell anyone if you did."

"No!" Heat flooded Virginia's face and she staggered back. "I wanted to see if Colleen had any leads on who might have taken my nail file. Whether someone is intentionally framing me or if they just saw it and took it."

Gemma seemed almost disappointed in Virginia's response. "Colleen's back in our room. She hasn't been feeling well," she said.

"Why did you hate the guy so much?" Virginia wanted to know. "I mean, he was an ass, but he seemed like a run-of-the-mill ass to me. Did he do something to you?"

Gemma shook her head, already turning back toward the event hall for another game. "I'm just glad the world is down one awful man. Now, I've got more money to win."

* * *

COLLEEN. Virginia knew she needed to talk to her psychic friend. Her cryptic visions hadn't been wrong yet, and the more time passed, the more agitated Virginia felt.

She turned back down the hallway with their rooms. Hers and Marney's was first, followed by Dick's, then Liam's. On the other side of the hallway was Patricia's, and further down were Kim's, Russ's, and finally Gemma's and Colleen's shared room. The tournament was popular, and they hadn't been able to get rooms all together. Virginia made her way down the hall toward Colleen, a sense of dread filling her the further down the hall she went. When she came to Russ's room, she paused. Her heart drummed in her ears. The door was cracked, left open by the police as they'd gone in and out earlier that morning.

She knew she shouldn't. She knew it was a bad idea. But Virginia stepped forward and pushed the door open, then slipped inside the room.

The first thing Virginia noticed was the made bed. Russ was either a neat freak or hadn't slept there the night before. Her eyes drifted from the neat corners of the bed to the carpet on the other side of the bed, between it and the door to the bathroom. A deep reddish-brown stain covered the carpet. Evidence tags were placed on the floor.

She stifled a gag, clenching her fists, and tore her eyes from the sight.

The rest of the room was neat. A briefcase sat on the lone chair in the corner. Virginia started to make her way to it but tripped, catching herself on the chest of drawers. She was steadying herself when the door opened and she whirled around, hand to her chest. Marney stood in the doorway looking horrified.

"What are you doing in here?" she hissed. Her eyes were wide, and Virginia could tell in that moment that Marney wasn't sure of her innocence. She felt suddenly as if the air in her lungs was lead. When Virginia couldn't respond, Marney stepped fully inside the room and shut the door behind her, making sure it was properly closed. "I was pacing, trying to loosen up my legs, and then I heard something inside Russ's room. And then *you're* in here? The prime suspect, and you think it's a good idea to be sneaking around in the dead guy's room? Are you insane?"

"I'm sorry!" The words came out louder than Virginia intended. Her eyes cut over to the door before returning to Marney. She lowered her voice. "I was going to talk to Colleen. Gemma said she was in their room. But then I came to Russ's room and the door wasn't closed all the way, and then…" The stupidity of what she'd done hit her. "We should go."

Marney looked around before saying anything, stunning Virginia. "We're here already, aren't we?"

Virginia nodded.

"And you didn't kill Russ." A statement, not a question.

Virginia could have cried with relief. She shook her head instead.

Marney sighed. "We might as well have a look around while we're here."

Her friend was extending her a lifeline. Virginia grabbed on.

The two women started poking around. Virginia pulled open the drawers in the dresser one by one, while Marney moved to the bathroom and pulled open the medicine cabinet. Nothing. They moved to Russ's suitcase, a weekender bag half-zipped and sitting at the foot of the bed. They looked pointedly away from the blood-stain on the carpet as they made their way around the room. Virginia knelt, gripping the mattress to help ease herself down onto her knees, then unzipped the bag the rest of the way. The dark leather of the bag smelled divine as she leaned toward it. She wondered how much a bag like this must have cost, the material smooth as silk under her fingers.

Inside were a handful of shirts, a pair of pants, and a few sets of boxer briefs. She pulled one of the latter out of the bag, then dropped it on the floor upon realizing what it was, as if it were scalding. Marney giggled, and Virginia turned. Her friend had become so anxious, worse even than she'd been when she and Dylan first escaped to Seaview, and the sound of her laughter felt like music to Virginia. Like hope.

The moment was short-lived. There was a shuffling sound in the hallway outside the door, followed by the click of the lock unlatching and the turn of the door handle. Marney and Virginia stared in horror as the door opened and a figure stepped into the room.

Kim.

The nurse jumped back, as startled to see Virginia and Marney in the room as they were to see her. "What are you two doing in here?" she demanded.

"We, um," Marney started to stammer out a response but came up with nothing.

"*You.*" Kim's voice was venomous as she turned to Virginia.

Virginia instinctively put her hands up in the gesture of surrender before gripping the bed to pull herself back to her feet.

"I know it was you. I know it was yours." Fury was written on Kim's face. She took an angry step toward Virginia. Virginia stepped to the side in front of Marney.

"Why do you have a key to Russ's room?" Virginia was surprised her voice didn't waver. She sounded far more confident than she felt, and it made her straighten up an inch taller and thrust her chin up.

But Kim was unfazed. "You're not going to turn this on me, murderer." She spat the last word, and Virginia flinched. So much for appearing confident. "Now get out."

It didn't matter that it wasn't Kim's room. Virginia and Marney eagerly obeyed, nearly tripping over each other as they made their way out the door and down the hall. Virginia could feel the searing gaze of Kim's watchful eyes the entire way down the hall.

* * *

"WHAT WAS SHE DOING IN THERE?" Virginia finally asked. Back in their room, she and Marney had stood in shell-shocked silence until Virginia couldn't take it anymore.

Marney shrugged, picking up her crochet hook and busying her hands.

"Do you think that detective is still here?"

At that, Marney looked up. Her eyes widened slightly. "You're going to go talk to the police?"

"Is it that hard to believe?" But Virginia knew it was. How many times had she begged Marney to investigate the murders earlier that spring instead of going to the police? "I just think he should know Kim was sneaking around in there. She found him, after all. And she had a key!"

"He gave me his card," Marney said. She picked up a small, cream-colored business card from the side table and handed it to Virginia. Beneath the police department logo was a name and a title. Aaron Foster, Lead Investigator. And beneath that, a phone number.

Virginia thanked her and clutched the card in her

fingers. It felt significant. Like the card somehow contained the essence of the detective, and in her hand she held either her salvation or her damnation. "I'm going to go see if he's still around. If he's not, I'll call him."

The detective wasn't anywhere to be found. Not in the dining room, the main atrium, the event hall, or the casino floor. Virginia made a final lap around the floor, the nervous fluttering in her stomach increasing in intensity. She spied Patricia at a slot machine, but no detective. She turned to leave, deciding she'd step outside into the parking lot to make the call. She needed the fresh air. But as she stepped outside and rounded the corner, she collided with a tall figure.

The man cursed. "Watch where you're going!"

When she stepped back, Virginia could see that the man she'd run into was the detective.

"Detective Foster," Virginia said. "I am so sorry."

"You again." He narrowed his eyes, and Virginia considered turning and leaving without saying anything. But Kim's face upon seeing her and Marney in Russ's room flashed in her mind, and she steeled herself.

"I was actually looking for you. I have some information about Russ's murder."

Detective Foster raised an eyebrow but said nothing.

"I saw Kim in Russ's room earlier. She had a key."

The detective nodded, taking in the information. "When did you see her?"

"Five or ten minutes ago."

"And did you see what she was doing?"

"No, she just came in and then looked all surprised, like she'd been caught."

"She came in? As in, you were also in Russ's room?"

"I, well—" Virginia knew she'd made a mistake. "I walked past, and the door wasn't shut all the way. I looked in to see what the deal was, and then Kim came."

"And she had a key?"

Virginia nodded.

"So you were in the victim's room, and then someone else entered Russ's room, and you think we should scrutinize that person for it but overlook your presence at the crime scene?"

Virginia felt herself shrink before him.

"I suggest," the officer continued, "that you stay away from the crime scene. I'd say that's a pretty good rule of thumb: stay out of crime scenes."

"Will you at least look into Kim?"

"Bring me evidence, not gossip. Then we'll talk."

Detective Foster turned to walk away, and before she could stop herself, Virginia asked, "Will I get my nail file back?"

The detective turned to look her up and down and barked out a laugh. "Implicated in a crime, and you're asking when you can get the murder weapon back? That's a first for me." His sharp features took on a threatening quality as he looked at Virginia with incredulity. He turned and continued his walk away from Virginia, back to where two other officers stood by a group of police cars in a corner of the parking lot. Over his shoulder, he called, "I'd suggest you get a new nail file. Maybe one that's less recognizable."

CHAPTER 5

Reeling from the detective's harsh dismissal and feeling like a fool for expecting a different response, Virginia pulled open the door and let the air conditioning wash over her before making her way to Colleen's room. Tears prickled at her eyes, threatening to fall, and she bit her tongue and thrust her shoulders back. Maybe she could trick her mind into feeling an ounce of confidence.

The door to Russ's room was firmly closed as she walked past it. Virginia averted her eyes, frustration burning in her core as she passed. When she arrived at the door to Colleen's and Gemma's room she knocked harder than she intended. Each strike of her fist against the wood felt like a small relief.

No answer.

She knocked again. "Colleen! It's Virginia!"

Still nothing.

Defeated, Virginia leaned her back against the door. She knew if she returned to her own room she wouldn't be able to stop herself from venting and decided to spare Marney the stress. Gemma's coldness was off-putting enough that Virginia was in no hurry to talk with her again, but she thought Ronald's sense of humor might ease the anger and irritation barely masking the terror lurking under the surface. The fear that she wouldn't be believed, that her forgetfulness, her inability to keep track of her belongings, might cost her everything. Hours ago, she was worried solely about losing her spot in Breeze Village. Suddenly things seemed much more dire.

She shook the thought from her mind and started toward the event hall in search of Ronald. The room was packed. Nearly every table was full, and Virginia strained behind her glasses but couldn't make out Ronald in the sea of people. She took a seat at a table in the back. With no good options, what hurt could a round of bingo do? Maybe she'd get lucky.

Virginia studied her card, but when she raised her head to look toward the caller on the podium, the face she saw across the table from her made her breath catch in her throat. There, across the table, was Kim.

Instead of a grimace, Kim's face looked entirely absent of emotion. Her eyes were swollen and red, rimmed with dark purple underneath. Her cheeks were red and blotchy, and the skin on the underside of her nose had been rubbed so raw it was nearly bleeding. The tears had stopped, but a vacant expression had replaced the anguished one Virginia had seen in the dining room.

Did she look this bad in Russ's room? Virginia had been so caught off guard, so panicked, that she hadn't noticed. And Kim had been angry, vicious. Whether she looked like she'd been held underwater and then dragged behind a truck had not been Virginia's primary concern.

Virginia waited for Kim to make a snide remark, to attack, to ask Virginia why she was staring at her. But she didn't. And something about those reddened eyes, the unseeing expression, brought a wave of sympathy rising up in Virginia. She'd known loss, and this was a person experiencing loss.

"Are you okay?" Virginia asked, unable to stop herself.

Kim turned to look at her, and her eyebrows knit together slightly. The faintest hint of emotion. "No."

Unsure of what else she expected, Virginia tried to think of what she could say to comfort the nurse. Kim was suspicious, but she was also clearly grieving. "I know what you're feeling," she started but stopped herself when Kim screwed up her face in response.

"Oh, you know what it feels like to be sitting next to a possible murderer who won't leave you alone during one of the worst moments of your life?"

Virginia looked back down at her bingo card. "I just meant that this spring, the Breeze Village murders: I found those bodies. I know how shocking and upsetting it is."

Kim let out a dark laugh. "I've found plenty of bodies. You don't make it long in this profession without encountering a few. They're just not normally brutalized by a crazed old woman."

Kim's barbs cut through the last of Virginia's sympathy and she looked up, fixing her eyes on Kim's. "I know you're hurting, but I did not kill Russ."

"I heard you arguing, remember? 'You're going to

regret this decision.' Ring any bells?" She cocked an eyebrow, challenging Virginia, and Virginia's stomach sank. She'd forgotten about the exchange. Kim let out another breathy laugh, and Virginia tried to compose her face, to look less surprised, less afraid. "That's what I thought." Kim looked away, clearly finished with the conversation.

"I16." The game continued. It was blackout bingo, and Virginia had half the card covered. She hated blackout bingo. It took so long for someone to win. She shifted uncomfortably in her chair.

"When did you last see Russ?" Virginia was half surprised by the question even as she heard herself ask it.

Even more surprising was that Kim deigned to respond. A shrug. "When everyone else did."

Virginia waited, unsure what that meant. The silence between them dragged on, interrupted by the rhythmic calling of letters and numbers, the tiny thrill when Virginia was able to fill in another square. Two-thirds covered now.

"I saw him at dinner," Kim continued, unprompted. "Then I went to my room. He was on the phone when I left the dining room. That was the last I saw of him until…"

The two winced in unison.

"You didn't leave your room after dinner?"

"I said I didn't see Russ again. Not that I didn't leave my room. I don't know why I'm answering your questions, anyway."

Virginia backed off. A tiny bead of hope was forming. Kim had found Russ. Had a key to his room. There was something here, and she was talking openly to Virginia about it.

"I went to the bar later in the evening. Dick was there, laughing with some guy. He's a real social guy, Dick. Hobbles around with that walker, but he's got more energy than a lot of people half his age. But Russ wasn't there. And then I went to my room, and after I came out for breakfast I went to check in on Russ since he wasn't there, either, and that's when I found him."

When Kim finished talking, she was almost panting, as if telling her story had been a physical feat. Virginia thought she looked lighter, unweighted, if only a little.

"Your room is next to Russ's, right? You didn't hear anything last night?"

Kim shook her head.

"And when you found him, was there anything else weird or out of sorts? Anything that caught your eye?"

As soon as she'd said it, Virginia knew she'd gone too far.

"Other than your nail file lying in the pool of his blood?" Kim stood as she spoke, her voice raising. The caller looked up from his spot on the podium, alarmed. As all eyes turned to them, Virginia's cheeks flushed, and Kim's incensed expression softened with a hint of embarrassment. Before Virginia could respond, Kim was hurrying from the room.

"O64," the caller said, confusion in his voice.

Across the room, someone called, "Bingo!"

Virginia counted to twenty-five in her head before following Kim out of the room. She didn't want to face the nurse again, but she wanted to be out of that ballroom full of curious eyes as quickly as possible. In the open space of the atrium, Virginia felt like she could breathe again. But with the first deep breath, she felt herself shake and start to cry.

Caught off guard, Virginia tried to hurry back to her room. She wanted to find Marney. She wanted a hug. She wanted comfort and guidance on what to do next. But her legs protested as she began yet another trek across the atrium, through the dining room, down the hall.

As she rounded a corner, she found herself face-to-face with Ronald. At the sight of Virginia, he broke into a wide grin, his eyes twinkling.

"Well, well, well, I hear it's your turn to be accused of murder." Laughter danced in his voice.

He meant it in jest, but Virginia had to bite down on her tongue to keep him from seeing her cry. Though she'd received recognition for solving the murders of Ruth, Genie, and Byron in the spring, the residents of Breeze Village remembered the dead ends she ran down, the accusations she levied in her pursuit of the truth.

His smile drooped when he saw Virginia's reaction, and he took a step toward her to wrap her in a hug. He was a short man—Virginia swore he'd shrunk even in the few months she'd known him—and she rested her chin on the top of his head in their embrace. She regretted that she ever thought he might be capable of murder. She hated that people could think that about her now.

"We know you didn't do it, Virginia," Ronald said, pulling back from their hug.

Virginia mumbled a thanks and continued on her way, unable to stop the tears and needing to be alone.

To her surprise, Marney wasn't in their room when Virginia arrived. A surprising number of crocheted works covered every surface. How had Marney done so much so quickly? But Marney was gone.

Virginia splashed water on her face and then lowered herself onto the bed, groaning. Her body ached. She suddenly felt exhausted. She lay back, staring at the ceiling, then closed her eyes. She breathed in for four counts, then out for six. When she opened her eyes, the light pouring into the room was golden, and her stomach rumbled.

Groggy, she looked around her. Still no Marney.

At the urging of her stomach, she slipped her sneakers back on, brushed the post-nap slime from her teeth, and set out in search of food. The restaurant off the casino floor was a neon-lit spectacle of flaming desserts, drunk patrons dancing on one another, and high-rollers showing off by buying drinks for their friends. And there, in the center of it all, was the Breeze Village crowd. Gemma spun Ronald on the dance floor while Dick used his walker as a partner, spinning and dipping himself right alongside them. Marney and Colleen sat in a booth, faces close together, smiles brightening both of their expressions. Marney sipped a soda, and Colleen seemed to be sipping something stronger.

"Hi." Virginia felt out of sorts sliding into the booth next to them, like an outsider joining the party.

"She wakes!" Marney beamed at Virginia, and she felt her muscles relax ever so slightly.

"She needs food," Virginia replied. Colleen slid a basket of lukewarm fries toward her, and Virginia took several in her fingers, stuffing them in her mouth greedily before regretting it upon tasting them.

"The guest of honor!" Gemma sidled over, sliding into the booth beside Virginia, her large frame compressing Virginia and Marney against the wall. When the three stared at her in confusion, Gemma gestured toward Virginia. "Our murderess. Asshole men everywhere cower in fear of her nail file."

The french fries threatened to come back up, and Virginia battled to keep them down. Mercifully, neither Marney nor Colleen laughed.

"Ronald already made that joke," Virginia said when she felt confident she could speak without her stomach emptying itself. "It's lost some of its charm on the second take, I'm afraid."

"Speaking of asshole men," Colleen said quietly, eyes floating upward toward someone at the other end of the room. Virginia, Marney, and Gemma turned in unison to see Liam striding toward them, face drawn. He looked entirely uncomfortable in the restaurant. With each new corner of the room he regarded, his frown deepened. By the time he arrived at their table, the corners of his mouth were near to reaching the bottom of his jaw. He looked positively repulsed.

"We're leaving tomorrow," he said shortly. "After breakfast."

Relief blossomed in Virginia. Just a few more hours

and they'd be away from this place. From the looks on their faces, Marney and Colleen agreed. Gemma, on the other hand, poked out her bottom lip.

"What about the rest of the tournament?" she whined.

"Given the circumstances, I've decided it's best we return home."

Liam didn't give Gemma a chance to further object, turning on his heels and practically running from the room.

"Well, I'd better make the best of what time we've got left here." Gemma planted her hands on the table and pushed herself up, arms jiggling with the motion. Virginia and Marney spread out, able to breathe with the newly relinquished space. Gemma sidled over to the bar, and Virginia saw her down two tiny glasses of clear liquid, shake her head vigorously, then return to the dance floor, where she promptly embraced a stranger and began to lead him in a dance.

"She should have retired here," Colleen said, smiling as she watched Gemma and her partner leap and spin across the cramped dance floor.

But Gemma was like this everywhere. Always the life of the party, radiating joy anywhere she went. The song changed, and a country hit blared over the speakers. Virginia ordered a hamburger but it tasted like ash on her tongue. She willed herself to chew and swallow. Just a few more hours, she reminded herself. A few more hours and she'd be home. Whatever that meant.

* * *

THE CASINO and its adjoining restaurant only became more lively as the night went on, and the joyous merriment of the gamblers mixed with the heaviness of the greasy hamburger made Virginia's stomach churn. She excused herself, surprised that Marney wanted to stay and continue talking with Colleen. It stung that her friend wanted to spend time with someone else—the psychic who was happy to sit in a loud, chaotic restaurant but was feeling unwell when Virginia needed her help. Virginia pushed those thoughts down, didn't let herself think them as she plodded back to her room.

She regretted the nap she'd taken. Her grogginess had fully bled into grumpiness, and she knew sleep wouldn't find her for hours if she returned to her room. The last rounds of bingo had concluded for the day. The night stretched ahead of her, daunting. Hours of darkness to spend alone with her thoughts. *No, thank you.*

As she walked by Russ's room, she heard the detective's words from that afternoon. "Bring me evidence, not gossip."

Though she'd poked around earlier, her investigation had been cut short. And with nothing more appealing to do in the hours laying before her, Virginia looked at that closed door and made up her mind. She needed to get back in there.

She jiggled the handle, the metal cool in her fist. Locked, of course.

She pulled her own room key from her pocket. An idea.

The ding from the small metal bell atop the front desk carried throughout the lobby. An attendant appeared, his crisp uniform at odds with his unruly beard and tangled shoulder-length hair. Virginia could smell him from across the desk. It was a considerable effort to keep herself composed.

"My key isn't working," she told him. She spoke from her throat, ensuring her voice wobbled a bit, and gripped the counter, sagging into it. "I went to turn in for the night, and I can't get into my room."

To her delight, the clerk, who couldn't have been older than twenty-three, looked terrified. No one wanted an elderly woman to face-plant in the main lobby on their shift, nor did they want to be the ones keeping said elderly woman locked out of her room when she looked ready to collapse at any moment.

"Let me help you," he said, taking her key. "What room number is it?"

Virginia screwed up her face as if struggling to remember the number when in reality, she'd written it on her hand. Old, she may be. But she had her systems.

"It's 103," she said finally. "Yes, that's it. Room 103."

The attendant went to work activating a new room key for her, face serious, as if it was the most important task he might take on that evening. Virginia almost felt sorry for duping him. Almost.

She accepted the key from him, letting her hand tremble as she took it, and turned back toward the hall where her room and, more importantly, room 103 waited. It wasn't until she heard the door to the back office slam behind the attendant that she let herself straighten up and walk at full speed.

Standing in front of Russ's room, Virginia took a deep

breath. She looked around and, after making sure the hallway was clear, held the key to the handle. A green light. A click. And she was in.

The coppery smell of blood met Virginia's nose first. Copper and leather and expensive cologne. She placed a hand against the wall to steady herself, fully looking the part of a fragile eighty-year-old, barely keeping herself together now that she was alone in the room.

This is a mistake. I shouldn't be here.

She turned to exit, hand on the cool metal of the handle, but a sound made her jump and whirl around. Her eyes went wide, and she took in the space. No one was there. But the sound continued. A low pulsing, coming from one of the drawers in the bedside table.

Virginia crept over to it, heart pounding, and pulled open the drawer. Inside were a handful of books. She picked up the top one. *The Intelligent Investor.* Then the next. *The God Delusion.* She shuddered. She reached for the last book, a thick copy of *Atlas Shrugged.* It was vibrating. She flipped open the cover to find that the book had been hollowed out, concealing a small hiding place. Nestled inside were three phones, one of which was lit up and buzzing. Across the screen, the words "unknown caller."

Virginia picked up the phone and answered it but said nothing.

From the other end of the line came ragged breathing, then a gulp. "Hello? Who is this?" A woman's voice, raw and angry.

Virginia said nothing. She wasn't sure she could get the words out even if she knew what to say. She willed herself to quiet her breathing, to slow her heart rate as the thrumming threatened to drown out the voice on the phone.

"Is this his wife? Or are you one of the other floozies waiting for him to leave her? News flash: he's not going to. The lying bastard." The woman on the other end of the line sounded crazed. Her voice raised with every word. Then, quieter, almost scared: "How did you get this phone?"

The line went dead.

Virginia reached into the drawer and pulled out the other two phones. All were locked, requiring a fingerprint to get inside. But they were evidence. Three phones, tucked inside a secret cavity concealed in a book. Russ clearly had something to hide. And whoever was on the other end of that line was angry. Virginia wondered how many "floozies" there were, how angry they might be if they found out they weren't Russ's only. Angry enough to kill him?

Steps drew closer outside the door. The handle jiggled. Virginia stood frozen to the spot, heart caught in her throat. The handle stopped jiggling. Ease began to settle over Virginia, but before she could even turn back to look at the phones in her hand, she heard shuffling, then the door latch unlocked.

CHAPTER 6

Without thinking, Virginia turned and shoved herself into the closet, tucking herself into the dark corner behind a suit Russ had hung up.

The door opened, and Virginia heard footsteps in the room. Panic flooded her. Had the mystery woman on the other end of the line come to see who had Russ's phone?

Virginia reassured herself that it wasn't possible. Whoever was on the phone wouldn't be able to get here so soon, likely wouldn't know where Russ was staying if he treated his side pieces as poorly and told them as little about his life as Virginia suspected.

Virginia tried to focus, to think of a plan, to figure out who might be in the room with her. Her brain felt empty, devoid of coherent thought and filled instead with a loud ringing, thick static. The heavy musk of Russ's cologne lingering on his suit mixed with the copper scent of the blood on the carpet, and Virginia thought she might gag and give herself away. Then the thought that whoever was in the room with her might be Russ's killer found her, and any hope of coming up with a solid plan left her. All she could think about was that she had been nosy, determined to find evidence herself instead of leaving it to the police, and now she might have trapped herself in a room the size of a shoebox with a murderer.

Virginia heard a low grunt, the sound of a mattress being lifted and thumping back down into place, followed by the sounds of drawers opening, contents hitting the floor. Whoever was here was looking for something. Virginia dared half a peek around the suit but pulled herself back out of sight before she could catch a glimpse of the intruder. They had a key. Virginia wondered if it could be Kim.

The steps got further away as the person padded toward the bathroom. Sounds of the medicine cabinet opening and shutting, the bathroom cabinets and drawers being yanked open and slammed shut, made Virginia wince. Then the steps drew nearer again, and Virginia pulled her own phone from her pocket. She could text Marney, have her come cause a commotion to draw the intruder out. The intruder stalked toward the door, and just when Virginia thought they would leave, her own phone buzzed in her hand.

The steps stopped.

Then drew closer.

Virginia tucked herself as close to the wall as she could, making her breath as shallow and silent as she could.

The closet doorknob turned excruciatingly slowly, letting out a low creak as a shaft of light began to shine through the crack. An inch. Two inches. The door was nearly half-open. Virginia's heart was thumping so loudly in her ear, she wondered if the intruder could hear it. The light coming in through the opening door grew closer and closer to where Virginia's sneakers poked out from behind Russ's suit.

Just as it reached the tips of her shoes, illuminating her toes, a shrill ring startled Virginia so much that she jumped slightly, jostling the suit concealing her. Virginia readied herself to be caught, to be held up at gunpoint and disposed of by the murderer who'd come back to find whatever they hadn't taken when they'd slaughtered Russ. But the intruder was also startled by their own phone ringing and jumped, bumping the closet door and sucking in a gasp of air. The ringing was silenced, and the intruder padded away from the closet, hurrying from the room. Virginia counted to fifty before she dared to move, then could only slump down against the wall, hugging her knees in the corner of the closet where she'd been so sure she was about to be killed.

When the seconds ticked on and the intruder didn't return, Virginia twisted to grip the wall and pull herself back to standing, knocking the suit entirely off its hanger in the process. After extracting herself from the closet, she picked up the jacket, the charcoal wool soft in her fingers, and returned it to its place. She turned to leave but turned back and plunged her hands into the suit pockets.

The jacket pockets were empty. She tried the pants pockets. They were also empty. In the name of being thorough, she pulled at the fabric of the jacket and searched for an interior breast pocket. As Virginia slid her fingers inside, they met something that felt like a credit card. Virginia curled her fingers around the thick plastic and pulled it from the pocket. It was a hotel key. Not to the casino hotel where they were staying, but someplace out west, it seemed. The front of the card depicted a white stucco resort, all balconies and interconnected outdoor stairwells with palm trees interspersed and mountains in the background. On the bottom of the card in white script was the name *The Royal Marina.*

Virginia pocketed the key, then patted her pockets to make sure the three phones she'd retrieved earlier were still there. Then, as hastily as she could urge her legs to carry her, she left Russ's room and returned to her own, where she found Marney crocheting in the lone armchair by the window.

"Where were you?" Marney hardly looked up from her work as she asked the question, but Virginia could hear the edge to the words. The panic. Marney had returned to their room expecting to find her best friend and instead found it empty.

In answer, Virginia pulled the phones from her pockets and laid them on the table beside Marney one by one. "I found these in Russ's room."

Marney's eyes grew wide, and she shook her head as she looked up at Virginia. "You shouldn't have gone back. You could have been caught! Do you realize how it would look if someone found you at the crime scene a second time?"

Virginia decided not to tell Marney about her close

call. It would only upset her, send her into a further panic, and there was nothing to be done about it now. "I know," Virginia said softly. "But the detective wouldn't listen to me without evidence. Now we've got evidence."

Marney picked up one of the phones, turning it over in her hand, then set it down quickly as if it had burned her. "So you're going to call the detective back now? Turn these in?"

Virginia looked over at the clock on the nightstand between their beds. Ten o'clock. "In the morning." She moved into the bathroom, then when the door was shut and locked behind her, she let herself dissolve a little. Her thin fingers gripped the cheap fake marble counter, knuckles white. The pearly pink nail polish she chose week after week looked severe against the pallor of her skin. When she looked up at herself in the mirror, her cheeks sagged, and her eyes looked heavy. Twenty-four hours ago, her primary concern was doing well enough at bingo to bribe an asshole to let her move into a retirement community with her best friend. Now that asshole was dead, and Virginia was the prime suspect.

She ran the shower hot. She'd always taken lukewarm showers, keeping her hair from the water as much as possible to preserve her style. She'd heard somewhere that hot water was bad for the skin, and especially bad for the hair, and once her hair had started to thin, she'd decided to take no chances. But today, her hair was not a concern. Washing the stress, fear, and judgment of the day away was the only thing on her mind as Virginia stepped into the scalding water and scrubbed and scrubbed.

Marney was already in bed when Virginia emerged from the bathroom, steam billowing out into the bedroom when she opened the door. Virginia tiptoed to her own bed in the dark and slid between the covers. Soon they'd be back in Seaview, and miles of physical space would separate her from this place and everything that had happened here.

"I love you." Marney's voice sounded tiny.

Virginia tossed her comforter back, feeling the heavy weight of grief and guilt threatening to crush her. Though she hadn't killed Russ, she was the reason they were all there. And she was the reason Marney was so broken. Soon, she reminded herself, they'd be back in Seaview. Back home.

"I love you, too."

Exhaustion overcame Virginia and she clung to it, yearning for the sweet relief of unconsciousness, willing herself to sleep.

* * *

IT WAS STILL DARK when Virginia awoke, heart already racing. She peered over at the clock on the bedside table and squinted to make out the numbers. Five in the morning, on the dot. She rolled over, knowing she wouldn't find sleep again but wanting to let Marney sleep for as long as possible and not eager to get out of bed and face the day ahead of her.

"I'm awake, too." The covers on Marney's bed swished as she rolled over to face Virginia.

"Why are you awake?"

"Bad dream."

They lay in silence in the dark for a few minutes before Marney moved again. "Thanks for telling me," she said. "About the phones."

The meekness of her voice made Virginia want to cry. Her best friend, and here she was, thanking Virginia for sharing a huge piece of information with her as if it were an unexpected grace. Virginia had been so closed off—was still so closed off, keeping the secret of how she'd nearly been caught from Marney—and usually she could tell herself it was for the best. But Marney's soft thanks for opening up cracked her open. Virginia's eyes stung, and her breath caught in her throat, and then she opened up further.

"There's more I didn't tell you."

Virginia pulled herself up on her elbow to face Marney. Even in the dark, she could tell that Marney's eyes were wide and she was watching Virginia eagerly, ready to take it all in. And Virginia told her everything. Starting with the key.

"There's one more thing I found. This hotel key from someplace out west. It was in Russ's suit pocket."

"That doesn't seem like much compared to the phones. Those are definitely the bigger find."

"There's also someone else who wants something Russ has. Or had. Or something they think Russ might have had."

Virginia swore she could hear Marney gulp. "What do you mean?"

Her voice shook as Virginia recounted her near miss

the night before. She glossed over the fear she felt cowering in the corner of the closet, focusing instead on the intruder's actions. How they'd opened drawers and cabinets, tossing things on the floor, then left when their phone rang.

"Did you hear their voice?"

Virginia shook her head, lips tugging down in disappointment. "They didn't answer it."

Marney sat in silence, taking in what Virginia had just laid on her. Then—*brrrring!* Both Virginia and Marney jumped, then Marney reached over to the nightstand. "My phone. It's Dylan."

Virginia caught herself before she asked Marney not to share anything she'd just told her with Dylan. That would be too far. But as Marney answered the phone, Virginia waited with bated breath to see what she'd tell her daughter.

Dylan was the Assistant Chief of Police back in Seaview, and just a few months earlier she'd insisted over and over that Virginia stop investigating the Breeze Village murders and leave it to the police. When Virginia's investigation put Marney in danger, Dylan had been ready to cut Virginia out of her life forever. They'd only arrived at a sort of truce after arresting the killer.

"We're fine, we're fine," Marney was saying as she swung her legs over the side of the bed and pushed herself up to standing. On the other end of the line, Virginia could just barely hear Dylan freaking out. She marveled that Dylan hadn't called her yet to blast her for somehow entwining Marney in another dangerous situation.

But this wasn't her fault, Virginia reminded herself.

She hadn't done this. But maybe if she was less forgetful, if she'd kept better tabs on her belongings, her nail file wouldn't have become the murder weapon and she wouldn't be wrapped up in this at all. Wouldn't feel the need to poke around, to investigate. Wouldn't be putting herself in danger.

Marney stepped into the bathroom for some privacy, and Virginia flipped on the lights in the bedroom and pulled back the curtains to let the pink morning light into the room. When Marney finally opened the bathroom door and stepped back into the bedroom Virginia tried not to look at her expectantly. *She'll tell you what she's ready to tell you, when she's ready to tell you.* It's none of your business. Still, she struggled to school her expression into neutrality.

"I didn't tell her," Marney said. So much for a neutral expression. "Any of it. She's apoplectic, of course. Worried about me. I figured telling her you're the prime suspect wouldn't do anything to help, nor would bringing up your little investigation last night."

Virginia felt her shoulders drop away from her ears and let out a breath she hadn't realized she'd been holding.

"Since you're going to the police here with the phones and hotel key today, I figured Dylan doesn't need to know. It's not her jurisdiction, and hopefully, with some concrete evidence, the detective here will be able to figure out who all might have had it in for Russ."

"Thank you." Virginia turned to her suitcase, picking out an outfit for the day and beginning to fold and pack the remainder. She was content to let the topic go, to turn the focus of the conversation elsewhere and think of anything besides the daunting prospect of talking with the detective again, but she felt Marney's gaze on her and looked up to see her friend staring at her with a puzzled expression. "What?"

"I'm just trying to think of who it could have been. The killer, the intruder. Do you think it was the same person?"

"I'm not sure who else it would have been."

"Three phones. Some unknown number of girlfriends, plus a wife. Who knows how many shady business contacts. The roster of people who might have wanted Russ dead is one heck of a list."

Virginia paused. She hadn't considered the wife. "Do you think his wife knew about all the affairs?"

"You think she killed him?"

Virginia shrugged. "Don't they say it's always the spouse?"

"Besides the embarrassment of being cheated on, there's the promise of a life insurance payout and all of his money." Marney cocked her head to the side, considering, then straightened up and shook her head as if trying to rid herself of the idea. "But I'm sure the detective is already on it. The wife will be one of the first people they'll call up to question."

The detective. Virginia's salvation, if he could figure out who killed Russ. And her damnation if he decided it was Virginia and didn't look any further. His dismissive voice from the previous evening rang in her head, and she cringed thinking about how he'd react when she told him she'd been in Russ's room again. Maybe, she thought, feeling guilty for even thinking it, she wouldn't tell him just yet.

* * *

As Virginia and Marney made their way in silence to the dining room for breakfast, the detective walked past them, heading toward Russ's room with a woman who looked deeply displeased to be there. Not sad, Virginia thought, but inconvenienced. She wore a sharp navy skirt suit and her brown hair, so dark it was nearly black with not a gray in sight, was cut into a neat bob. A powdery floral scent emanated from her, so strong that Virginia was unable to stifle a cough.

As he passed them, the detective gave Virginia a curt nod, the corners of his mouth tugging downward.

"That has to be the wife," Virginia hissed when they'd made it out of earshot. "Who else would he be taking to Russ's room?"

Marney let out an exaggerated breath. "I thought I was being gassed. She wears even more perfume than Gemma."

Virginia giggled. "Well, she might have killed the bastard, but she wasn't the one poking around in his room last night. Our mystery intruder didn't smell like they'd just showered in eau de parfum."

The two joined the rest of the Breeze Village bunch in the dining room, helping themselves to the continental breakfast. Only Gemma was missing.

"Is Gemma playing another round in the tournament?"

But a glance at her watch told Virginia it wasn't yet

time for the first round to begin, and Colleen shook her head, a wry smile spreading across her lips. "I believe she's still enjoying her dance partner from last night."

Her peers talked about the previous day's tournament victories and losses, who was going home with the big bucks, but all Virginia could think about was what Detective Foster and Russ's wife were discussing down the hall. She wondered if he'd tell her that Virginia was a suspect. No. It would be against protocol to discuss potential suspects. But her curiosity only grew, and when the pair reappeared from down the hall, it was all Virginia could do to keep herself from running after them.

Marney leaned over to whisper to Virginia, "Now's your chance." Virginia gave her a questioning look, and Marney added, "To talk with the detective. Tell him what you found."

"You're right," Virginia said. She turned to the rest of the table and excused herself before hurrying to the door Detective Foster and Russ's wife had walked through only moments ago.

But when she stepped out of the hotel and into the thick summer air, shielding her eyes from the morning sun, she held back as she searched for her target. To her right, she saw the detective getting into a police car and pulling out of the parking lot. To her left, she saw Russ's wife doing the same. "Shit," she muttered.

As soon as the detective's car rounded the corner, Virginia took off through the parking lot, hobbling as quickly as she could convince her legs to carry her. She stepped in front of Russ's wife's car—a pristine white Mercedes—and held her hands up above her head.

"What the hell are you doing?" The woman rolled her window down and leaned her head out, sunglasses framing her eyes despite the early hour.

"You're Russ's wife, right?"

A tight-lipped nod in response.

"I just wanted to offer you my condolences."

"And you thought this was the appropriate time and place?"

Virginia started to step around the car toward the driver's side window but didn't step all the way out from in front of the car. It wasn't entirely clear to her that the woman wouldn't speed off at the first opportunity.

"I'm sorry, I don't even know your name." Virginia felt an urgency to talk with the woman, to feel her out, but standing there with the opportunity before her, she couldn't think of a single thing to ask.

"Cindy. Now, if you'll excuse me." Cindy stuck a manicured hand out her car window and gestured for Virginia to move out of the way. Virginia noticed the lack of a wedding ring, though her wrist was adorned with several bracelets and a purple stone glinted on her pinky finger.

"It's nice to meet you, Cindy," Virginia continued as if she hadn't just been dismissed. "As I said, I just wanted to offer you my condolences. I know what it's like to lose a husband. I met Russ briefly, and he seemed like an... err, a wonderful man. I'm going to be moving into Breeze Village soon."

"Yes, well." Cindy pulled down her sunglasses and looked Virginia up and down, lips pursed. If she knew about Virginia's status as a suspect, she didn't give it away. "The business will carry on, don't you worry."

Virginia's jaw dropped open slightly and she started to protest, to tell Cindy she wasn't worried about the future of Breeze Village, but before she could say anything, the little Mercedes was backing up away from her. Cindy cut the wheel hard and peeled out of the parking lot, speeding away.

CHAPTER 7

Returning to Seaview and Breeze Village felt like stepping out of a movie theater into the bright light of the outside world. Squinting, not entirely sure what time it is, reorienting yourself to real life. Except the last few hours—few days—*were* real life, no matter how much Virginia wished they weren't.

Climbing the wooden stairs and stepping into the main building at Breeze Village, Virginia could have been convinced that the last two days hadn't happened. Everything seemed exactly the same, except Michelle was working at a new desk in one corner of the lobby instead of in her office. Russ's office, now. Would it be hers again? Or Cindy's? Virginia hadn't been concerned for the future of Breeze Village, but Cindy's assurance made her feel less certain. *The business will carry on.* As opposed to what? Closing down?

The idea that Virginia's suggestion to take a field trip to a bingo tournament could have been the domino that resulted in the closure of Breeze Village made her throat burn. She gripped the back of one of the lobby's armchairs to steady herself. A hand brushed her back, and she turned to see Marney looking at her, concerned. Virginia flashed her a smile, or the best approximation of one she could manage, and straightened, following Marney out to her cottage.

Pancake greeted them at the door, offering a little mewl as Marney bent over to stroke his head.

"Do you think Dylan told my kids about the murder?" Virginia helped herself to a sweet tea from the fridge.

"If they haven't called you yet, no chance they know."

Fair point. If the kids knew, they'd have been at the hotel themselves. At the very least, her phone would have been ringing off the hook. She felt relief that they didn't know, but her stomach sank at the realization that now she would have to be the one to tell them.

Virginia sat down on Marney's couch, sinking into it and leaning her head back. She wanted to turn on the TV and distract herself until she couldn't put off going home to Jack's house any longer. She picked up the remote and flipped on the TV. House Hunters was on.

"It's our show." Virginia looked over and gave Marney a smile, but Marney was looking at her apologetically. "What?"

"I told Dylan I'd meet her for a late lunch when we got back."

And just like that, Virginia was out of distractions, out of procrastination tactics.

When she pulled into the driveway at Jack's and Stephanie's house, afternoon sunlight peeked through the Spanish moss dripping from the ancient live oak that stood in the center of the yard. Jack's car was already in the driveway when she arrived, but Stephanie's was gone. As she crossed the hard, thick blades of grass bending beneath her sneakers, Virginia tried to decide whether it would be better to tell Jack on his own or if she could wait until Stephanie returned. Her "everything will be okay" attitude was such a strong balance to Jack's tendency to assume the worst.

Jack was on the phone, pacing in the living room. His tie was loosened around his neck and the sleeves of his dress shirt were rolled up. His suit jacket lay draped over the arm of the couch. He was working, probably home between meetings that had him zigzagging across town. When Virginia entered the house and gave him a small wave hello, Jack faltered mid-sentence and raised an eyebrow, surprised to see her. Virginia turned down the hallway toward the guest room before he had a chance to question her arrival a day earlier than expected. Behind her she could hear Jack collecting himself and returning to his conversation.

When Jack knocked on the bedroom door fifteen minutes later, Virginia was pacing. She'd already splashed water on her face, brushed her teeth, and changed her clothes. When she was rid of anything left from that place, the weekend she longed to put behind her, she'd lain down across the comforter and stared at the ceiling. Then stood back up and took to pacing.

Her heart wouldn't slow. Her brain felt like it was going a million miles a minute, but she couldn't nail down a single thought. It was running haywire but with nothing to show for it. No plan, just panic.

Jack knocked again, then turned the knob and entered. His eyes were wide, and worry was written across his face.

"You didn't answer when I knocked."

Virginia turned to face him, and the words fell out of her. "Someone killed Russ, and now I'm a murder suspect, and I might not have anywhere to go."

Jack took a step backward, staggering with the surprise of his mother's news. Virginia faced him, longing for him to step forward and wrap her in a hug, but instead, he put a hand on the door frame, steadying himself, maintaining the distance between them.

"But you didn't do it." A statement, but not with complete certainty. Virginia felt her heart break as she shook her head no. "Then we'll figure this out."

"I need to get some air." Virginia pushed past her son and left the house. She didn't know where to go. She just set off walking. By the time her legs protested and she called Lawrence to come pick her up, she felt better. When he didn't ask any questions, just drove her around Seaview until she was ready to go home, she thanked the heavens for him. And when she walked into the house and straight to the guest room and shut the door, Jack didn't follow her. Though Virginia knew he was probably on the phone with Lucy, working on a plan to prove her innocence, she breathed a sigh of thanks that he was leaving her alone.

* * *

VIRGINIA DIDN'T SEE Marney or Lawrence for the next two days. She avoided Jack and Stephanie, but with few places to go, it was difficult. With summer in full swing, even her favorite lesser-known beach spot wasn't the solitary escape it was in the off-season. She floated on the waves, dug her toes into the sand, let the saltwater rush over her face and body and pull her out away from the shore. But even as the water stung her eyes and dried her skin and the briny scent flooded her nose, the ruckus of families playing on the beach tugged her from her solitude.

On the third day after their return to Seaview, Virginia and Marney were due to renew their driver's licenses. It had been over sixty years since they'd had to take either the written or the practical tests for their licenses. Seaview, along with a handful of neighboring cities and towns, had recently passed a new law requiring seniors to retake the exams every ten years to ensure the roads weren't full of seniors who couldn't see or remember the rules of the road. A candidate for the state Senate made repealing those laws one of her primary campaign points after being crushed by the senior demographic in the last election.

Virginia swung by Breeze Village to pick up Marney. Her breathing was unsteady as she pulled into the parking lot. She wasn't sure what to expect from her friend, and she hated the uncertainty. It all dissolved the moment Marney pulled open the passenger door and flung herself into the seat.

"Let's get this over with." Pink sequins adorned Marney's tunic shirt, hanging down over white cropped pants and glinting in the mid-morning sun. Matching lipstick rimmed her mouth as she gave Virginia a nervous grimace.

"Don't look too excited."

"It's just been so long since the last test. I haven't parallel parked in years! What if I've forgotten how?"

"You parallel parked just last month. I was with you. You tapped that cute little red Buick on the way into the spot *and* on the way out."

Marney grimaced and flicked Virginia the bird, and Virginia felt herself light up. She was with her friend, and things felt almost normal. Closer to normal than she had hoped.

The DMV was exactly as it always was—overcrowded and understaffed, with half the computers not working and the air conditioner fighting for its life against the heat radiating off the crush of bodies inside. Once they'd made it through the line to give a disgruntled worker their documents and get in the queue for the tests they had to take, Virginia and Marney scanned the room for two seats next to each other and made their way to the far corner.

Virginia had double-checked that she had her glasses with her that morning, along with plenty of snacks. Marney had brought along her crochet bag and was scarcely seated before she pulled out a hook and some yarn and got to work on a small patterned square. Her cottage was full of the small squares waiting to be seamed together into a blanket.

"How long until you open your shop?" Virginia knew Marney was anxious about opening her online store to sell her crocheted goods and usually shied away from the topic since she felt she had little to contribute.

"Not long enough," Marney said simply. Her eyes glanced around the room as her fingers worked. Virginia marveled at how Marney could crochet so quickly, without even keeping a constant eye on her work.

By the time Marney was called up to take her exams, both of them were sweaty and exhausted. They had moved from conversation to sitting in silence as they'd become progressively snippier the longer they were there. Marney's written test was first, and she followed a disinterested teen through the room to a computer where he explained the procedure to her.

Virginia turned her gaze to the television, where the local news was playing. The volume was silenced, and subtitles flashed across the bottom of the screen. A young woman in a tight-fitting dress was standing in a parking lot and speaking into a microphone. Virginia saw the words *Breeze Village* flash across the screen, but the subtitles were gone before she could read the rest. The woman turned and the camera panned behind her. She was standing in the parking lot of Breeze Village, the main building behind her, and Michelle was standing beside her.

Virginia stood and moved closer to the TV so she could read the words that moved too quickly across the bottom of the screen. Her heart thrummed in her ears. She was about to see Michelle tell the community about Russ's murder and Virginia's status as a suspect; she was sure of it. Instead, the subtitles that flashed underneath

Michelle's characteristically stern face told a different story.

Virginia could make out about every other sentence. Michelle announced that she'd recently discovered staff at Breeze Village were engaged in a clandestine system of kickbacks with local doctors. The doctors recommended Breeze Village to their patients as they grew older, and the nurses at Breeze Village made sure the residents saw those same doctors as often as possible, sometimes for scans, tests, and procedures that weren't truly necessary.

Virginia's gasp caught in her throat, and she strained her eyes as she tried to keep up with the pace of the subtitles. Michelle continued, and from what Virginia could tell, she was saying she wasn't sure how long these kickbacks had been going on, whether they stemmed from the new staff that recently joined under Breeze Village's new owner or whether they had been going on long before. Regardless, she assured the news anchor, she was unaware until now and would be cooperating fully with any investigation.

The news anchor turned back to the camera, her face a perfect picture of surprise and concern, and began to recap what Michelle had just announced.

Virginia staggered back to sit but bumped into the man seated behind her. "Hey, watch it!" The man wore a suit and gave off a *too important to be here* vibe. Virginia mumbled an apology and made her way on shaking legs back to the corner where she'd been seated before. She could just barely see Marney in the testing area, leaning in close to the computer screen in front of her, unaware of Michelle's announcement.

When Virginia was called back to begin her exam, Marney had already been escorted out to the parking lot to begin the road test. Virginia took her seat in front of a chunky, ancient laptop. Its fan whirred so loudly inside it that it sounded as if the thing were trying to take flight. She donned her glasses and began the exam. One by one, she identified road signs and read through hypothetical situations, selecting the best response. It felt like a mix of things so common anyone would know and things she'd never once encountered in over six decades of driving. She hoped the balance was in her favor.

During the road test, Virginia felt comfortable if distracted. Though her mind was on Michelle and Breeze Village and the shock of the announcement, the test was a simple lap around the neighborhood, and muscle memory served her as she eased into the parallel parking space to cap off the exam.

Virginia returned to the fetid, under-ventilated room and stood before a plain background for her new license photo. When she was handed her new license, she looked around the room for Marney, eager to tell her what she'd seen on the television, and found her friend looking glum a few rows from where they'd been sitting before.

"What's wrong?"

Marney looked up, cheeks flushing slightly. "I failed." She stood and hurried toward the door, eager to get outside. When they'd left the stifling heat of the building for the blistering heat of the parking lot, she continued. "My eyesight isn't what it was. I could hardly read any of the questions in the written exam."

"And the parallel parking?"

"About as bad as last time." Marney grimaced, and Virginia took her friend's hand in her own, giving it a gentle squeeze.

"Well, I know a good eye doctor I can recommend. That is, if he's not part of some shady kickbacks scheme."

Confusion spread across Marney's face. "What do you mean?"

Excitement bubbled in Virginia as she started to tell her friend about what she'd seen on the news, mixing with the uncertainty at what this meant for Breeze Village. This was one more bit of change and chaos for the community.

By the time they crossed the asphalt lot and reached Virginia's little Honda, Marney was peppering her with questions Virginia didn't know the answers to, and both were eager to get back to Breeze Village and see what the others knew. Virginia pulled her seatbelt across her and turned the key in the ignition. She let her foot off the brake and began to back out of the parking spot, but just as she started to pull forward, thunder clapped and the sky opened up. One of the summer thunderstorms that cropped up so frequently in the South.

Panic spread through Virginia and she pulled back into the spot before turning to Marney, apology and embarrassment written across her face.

Marney, used to Virginia's anxiety around driving in the rain by now, asked, "Can one of your kids come get us? I'd drive us, but without a license…" She trailed off, embarrassment flooding her own face.

Virginia tried Lucy first. She'd always had more patience for Virginia's anxiety about driving in the rain than Jack. Her phone rang and rang until it went to voicemail. Jack answered his on the first ring, but he and Stephanie were at a doctor's appointment. Marney pulled out her phone and called Dylan. The two sat in embarrassed silence as they waited for her to come pick them up.

* * *

DYLAN DIDN'T ASK any questions. Just pulled up, stepped out of her truck, and helped Virginia and Marney up into it. No one spoke as they pulled away from the DMV, and the squat, dirty building shrunk in the rear view mirrors. Eventually, Virginia couldn't hold it in anymore.

"Did you see Michelle's announcement?"

Dylan said she hadn't, so Virginia gave her the rundown: some of the Breeze Village staff had an arrangement with local doctors that resulted in the residents receiving unnecessary medical treatment to pad those doctors' pockets.

"I just can't believe it." Marney shook her head, lips pulling down in a tight frown.

Virginia frowned. "I can't think of why she'd go straight to the press like that. I mean, she sells Breeze Village, the new owner dies, and now right in the midst of all that chaos, she goes on TV exposing illegal activities there. Is she just trying to tarnish the reputation of a dead man?"

Marney cocked her head to the side. "But then why would she have sold Breeze Village to him if she hated him so much?"

"Money," Dylan answered.

Marney didn't look convinced. "Michelle loves Breeze Village. I mean, I know she hasn't always been at the top of our *favorite people* list, but she really cares about that place. It's her baby. I can't see her turning it over to someone she hated or didn't trust just for the money."

"Are you going to be part of the investigation into all this?" Virginia wanted to know.

Dylan shook her head. "That'll be federal. Not our jurisdiction."

Virginia considered that. "Do you think it could be tied up with Russ's murder? The illegal kickbacks, I mean?" Her mind flashed back to the hidden phones in Russ's hotel room. She wondered whether his deception was limited to his romantic endeavors or if it extended to his business practices.

Dylan only shrugged. "That's not our jurisdiction, either."

The three rode in silence a little longer. Marney pulled out her crochet and began to work.

"How can you crochet if your eyesight is so bad?" Virginia asked.

"I guess I go by feel more than anything." Marney's voice was quiet, and Virginia regretted the question.

"I know it's not your jurisdiction, but in the cases you've worked in your career, how true is that saying about how it's always the wife?"

Dylan cast a glance back at Virginia. "In murder cases, you mean?"

Virginia nodded.

Dylan shrugged. "It's a saying for a reason. Why do you want to know?"

It was Virginia's turn to shrug, to keep her information to herself.

Then Marney lifted her head and replied, "Russ was cheating on his wife."

Virginia winced.

"And how do you know that?" Dylan's tone was that of rebuke.

Shut up, shut up, shut up. Virginia stared at the back of Marney's head, willing her to stop talking, but her attempt at telepathic communication failed, and Marney continued. "Virginia found multiple phones of Russ's that he was trying to hide."

"Oh, did she, now?" Dylan's voice was laced with thinly veiled fury that Virginia was involving herself in yet another murder investigation. That Virginia was endangering Marney by getting involved.

Marney, still crocheting, continued, oblivious to Virginia's silent pleas that she stop. "One of them rang, so Virginia answered it. It was one of his mistresses. But the detective has them now, so he's probably already investigating the wife and looking into whatever numbers called those phones recently."

Virginia felt herself grow rigid at Marney's statement that she'd given the phones over to the detective. And this time, Marney picked up on her wordless communication.

"You didn't give them to the detective." It was a statement, not a question, as Marney turned in her seat and gave Virginia a disappointed look.

The words lodged in Virginia's throat, and all she could do was give a slight shake of her head.

"You will call the detective before you get out of this car, and you will turn those phones over to him as soon as possible, before you get yourself into more trouble." Also not a question. Dylan's instructions came out hard, and Virginia felt herself shrink into the leather seat, face flushed with shame.

* * *

DETECTIVE FOSTER WAS LESS than thrilled to hear from Virginia. He was even less enthused when she told him she had some evidence relating to Russ's murder that he might be interested in.

"Let me get this straight." The detective sounded barely restrained on the other end of the line. "You went sneaking around in Russ's room, then came to me telling me Kim was suspicious because she came into the room. The exact same thing you were doing. Then, after receiving strict instructions to stay away from the crime scene, you returned. You allegedly found some cell phones, although because you took them with you, there's no proof they were Russ's or that they were in his room at all. And then you kept them for days. Do I have that right?"

Virginia's voice was small as she confirmed the series of events.

Foster let out a sigh and told her he'd send one of his officers to retrieve the phones the next morning. "You're lucky I'm not charging you with obstruction of justice or spoliation of evidence."

The stupidity of her actions weighed on Virginia. She felt like vomiting.

Before she could stop herself, though, she found herself asking whether the officer had seen Michelle's announcement earlier. "She was on the local news talking about an illegal kickbacks arrangement with some of the Breeze Village staff and local doctors. I just wonder if somehow it's connected."

The detective grunted that he'd have his guys look into it. A flicker of pride ignited in Virginia.

"Tomorrow morning. The phones. And if I find out you're hiding anything else from me..." Detective Foster didn't have to finish his threat.

Satisfied with Virginia's phone call, Dylan hopped down out of the truck and opened Virginia's door for her without another word. She helped Marney down more gently, hugging her goodbye before pulling out of the lot and returning to her work.

Virginia turned to Marney, expecting an apology for all she'd revealed in the car. Instead, Marney pushed past Virginia and headed inside without a word.

"What's wrong?" Virginia chased after her.

"You lied to me." The pain in Marney's voice caught Virginia off guard, and she didn't chase after her friend as she walked away.

The regret lingered when Virginia woke the next morning. She rolled over, groggy and disoriented after a fitful night's sleep, and tried to forget the hurt in Marney's face. She thought she might sleep the day away.

If she could avoid consciousness, she could avoid pain. Or at least the brunt of it.

Three loud raps at the bedroom door wrecked her plans. Then Jack's voice barreled in. "Mom, there's a cop here asking for you. What's going on?"

Virginia yanked open the door, her weary scowl meeting her son's condescending face. "The usual," she muttered. "Just your murder suspect mother meeting a cop for breakfast on this typical Thursday morning."

CHAPTER 8

The officer sent to collect the phones from Virginia was tall and lanky and looked even less pleased to see her than Detective Foster had sounded on the phone the day before. Sweat glinted on his pallid forehead. Yellow and brown teeth peaked out from behind cracked lips as he grimaced, and Virginia tried not to openly show her disgust.

"Here," she said, thrusting her hand out, a plastic bag containing the three phones dangling from her fingertips.

The officer took the bag from her, and Virginia yanked her hand away as his fingers brushed hers. The officer turned and stalked across the yard to his squad car without another word, and Virginia was glad to see him go, even as a piece of her felt like it was breaking as she handed over the evidence she'd risked her life to get.

Her stomach roiled, and she breathed deeply, trying to calm it. *Even if Detective Foster hates me, he's not a bad guy. He wants to catch a killer. And when he does, my name will be cleared.* Virginia just hoped he could do it quickly. If handing over the phones helped him identify the murderer, it was worth it.

Still, she reached down into the pocket of her robe and wrapped her fingers around the cool, stiff plastic of the hotel key she'd kept for herself.

When Virginia turned back to the house and opened the door, Jack was standing in the entryway. His arms were folded across his chest, and Virginia felt herself grow immediately defensive as he looked at her like a parent looks at a wayward teen.

"What was that about, Mom?"

"I'm not getting into this with you." Virginia tried to shove past him, but she was too much smaller, and he held firm.

"You said you were a suspect. You didn't say you involved yourself in the investigation. So why are there cops turning up on my doorstep?"

Virginia stepped back, bringing her hand up and shoving her finger in Jack's face, ready to remind him who was the parent. It felt silly even as she did it, scolding her son in his own home, the home he'd graciously allowed her to live in for months. She shoved the feelings of shame down and opened her mouth to yell, but Stephanie stepped out of the kitchen and beat her to it.

"Stop it, please!" Her ponytail was frizzy, loose hairs falling down around her face, and she was wearing holey sweats and clutching a mug of hot tea like it was a life-giving elixir. "You two are stressing me out!"

Virginia ignored her, preparing to resume her fight with Jack, but he stepped away immediately. "You're right. It's not worth yelling over." He planted a kiss on

Stephanie's forehead and moved into the kitchen, making himself a mug of tea.

Virginia followed behind, stung by Jack's dismissal of their fight. By backing off, he'd won, and the frustration fizzled inside her without the outlet of an argument. She searched the cupboard for coffee but they were out. No matter, she'd make some at work.

She was halfway through putting on her makeup when her phone rang. The sudden noise made her jump, smearing mascara on her upper eyelid. She muttered a curse, then answered the phone. "Hello?"

Dr. DiMarco's voice greeted her on the other end of the line. "Virginia." It was the voice you used when you were about to tell someone something they didn't want to hear.

"Is everything okay? I thought I wasn't supposed to come in for another hour today, but I can be there as soon as—"

Dr. DiMarco cut her off. "Everything is fine. You had the schedule correct. It's just... Did you happen to watch the local news yesterday afternoon?"

Michelle's announcement. Dr. DiMarco was one of the doctors involved in the kickback scheme with Breeze Village. Virginia gripped the counter to steady herself, her stomach dropping as she considered that someone she'd trusted could have been involved.

When Virginia didn't say anything, her employer continued. "Times are a little uncertain for me right now, and with things the way they are... I just don't think I can keep you on right now."

If the understanding that Dr. DiMarco was receiving

kickbacks for prescribing unnecessary treatments to her friends had yanked the floor out from under her, the sudden loss of her job, her only source of income, ripped away the very foundation. The phone slipped from Virginia's hand and clattered on the floor. She staggered from the bathroom to the bed, kneeling beside it and resting her forehead on the mattress.

With the uncertainty in every other aspect of her life—would she be able to move into Breeze Village? Would she be moving into a federal penitentiary?—the two days a week she spent organizing Dr. DiMarco's business and greeting patients was the one piece of stability Virginia could count on. And now it was gone.

Anger rose up inside her. Anger that Dr. DiMarco wasn't who she thought he was. Anger that she was the one paying the price. Anger that Michelle hadn't just kept her mouth shut. That she'd sold Breeze Village in the first place. If Russ hadn't ever come to town, Virginia would be settled in Breeze Village by now, or at least nearing the top of the waitlist. And Michelle had been the one to bring him into her life, to topple everything she'd relied on.

Virginia's anger surprised her. She didn't know what to do with it. She pounded her fists on the bed, but her weak punches only made her feel more frustrated. Tears streaked down her face, creating black tracks on the side where she'd swiped on mascara.

She washed her face, a futile effort as tears continued to spill, and left the room. She had to get out of there. She ignored Stephanie's look of shock and concern as she slid on her sandals and grabbed her purse. She let the door slam behind her, but it felt childish and barely took the edge off the fury building up inside her.

Virginia drove and drove. She had no destination, just the need to go. She crisscrossed downtown, the pedestrians and other drivers giving her a target for her anger. Anyone going slower than Virginia was an idiot, and she yelled at them from the bubble of her car. Anyone going faster was an asshole, and anyone on foot was a dumb tourist who needed to get the heck out of her town.

By the time she reached the beach, Virginia's throat was hoarse from cursing other drivers and her chest heaved with exhaustion. Carrying her sandals, she let the water lick her feet as she walked along the ocean's edge. It was healing, the ocean. When she needed someplace to go, she always found herself there, letting the sea calm her, bring her back to herself.

When the anger subsided, she was left with a gaping sadness. She felt alone. More alone even than when she tried to face Bellemeade on her own when she faced losing her home and her independence. Because now, she'd lost them. She'd won; she'd solved the murders. And she was still living with her children, entirely at the mercy of others.

Michelle's decision to sell Breeze Village and her revelation of what was going on behind closed doors, they'd upturned her entire life. But the upheaval itself wasn't what hurt the most. It was the power others still had over her. The fact that someone else could make a single decision and rip the world out from under her.

* * *

VIRGINIA ATE alone in her room that night and was doing the same at breakfast the next morning when a knock at her door drew her attention from the bowl of cereal in front of her. Without waiting for an answer, Stephanie pushed the door open. Her eyes were concerned, and Virginia turned away, knowing her own were still swollen from the previous day's tears.

"Will you join us for breakfast?"

"I'm almost finished."

Stephanie frowned. "Come sit with us anyway?"

Something in her big chestnut eyes tugged at Virginia's heart, and she agreed.

Jack had scarcely sat down at the table, a mug of tea in front of him replacing his usual coffee, when he made her regret it. "Mom, we want to start by saying how much we love you."

Virginia looked from Jack to Stephanie. Jack was looking at Stephanie, and she gave a small nod. Heat rose in Virginia's cheeks at the realization that they'd talked about her and had planned whatever conversation they were about to foist on her.

"We want, first and foremost, for you to be happy and comfortable," Stephanie added.

"I don't have another binder. But we wanted to remind you that there are, well, there are other options out there. And while we know the situation right now isn't ideal—"

Virginia cut him off, holding her hand up. "Whatever this is, a binder would have been better. At least I can throw a binder back at you."

Jack's mouth tugged down in disappointment. Stephanie looked genuinely surprised, which surprised

Virginia in turn. Did she really expect this to go any differently?

"Mom, there's a lot of uncertainty right now. But someplace like Harbor Vale might be a good idea. With all the chaos in Breeze Village… I know you were really looking forward to moving in there, but maybe it's not the right option."

Stephanie cut in before Virginia could object, reciting her half of their prepared speech. "Or there's always in-home care. We can rent you a place, something small but with a nice garden, and make sure you still get the right level of help."

Virginia stood, her chair scraping against the hard-wood as she pushed it back, causing both Jack and Stephanie to wince. "You want me out. Message received."

Stephanie rushed to stop her. "No, it's not that. It's not that at all. We just want you to be happy."

Her daughter-in-law had always been a kind heart. More empathetic than her husband. She couldn't stand to upset people, but in that moment, Virginia didn't care. "Happy somewhere else. Someone else's problem. I got it."

Jack and Stephanie continued to protest as Virginia turned down the hall. "Save it. I'm late for the Garden Review anyway."

It was a half-lie. She wasn't late, but there really was a meeting that day. And if she was going to clean herself up and get to the grocery store in time to plate the bakery cookies to look like homemade before the meeting, she had to get going.

The Garden Review Society met at the Seaview Botanical Gardens. The gardens rivaled those of a big city, thanks to a wealthy donor and lots of retirees. The volunteers truly did a phenomenal job, and the Garden Review Society was excited to feature these gardens for the first time, complete with interviews with half a dozen of the volunteers who had played such a large role in shaping them.

Virginia arrived with a tray of shortbread cookies. No one would be fooled into thinking she'd made them herself, but to bring them in a cardboard box from the bakery would be admitting to the gaffe of bringing something store-bought. To plate them showed an attempt at making it look homemade, a recognition of the expectations, if a failure to meet them.

Gemma, for her part, brought something homemade for the first time. It would have been better had she not.

"I made cupcakes!" Virginia wondered how Gemma didn't drop her cake tray as she greeted each new arrival with an enthusiastic one-armed hug, the tray swaying dangerously in the other hand the entire time.

Virginia took one and looked it over nervously. She'd witnessed Gemma's newfound interest in baking first-hand and hadn't seen any indication of skill in the kitchen, only enthusiasm. But the cupcake looked like a cupcake, so she took a bite. It did not taste like a cupcake, and she forced a smile and suppressed a gag, choking it down. Jan entered at the same moment, and Virginia took the opportunity to turn toward her in greeting, using the moment as a chance to discreetly spit out the bite of cupcake—or salty cardboard masquerading as a cupcake.

"Virginia, it's so good to see you!" Jan's hair was piled atop her hair as usual and swayed as she bobbed across the room and wrapped Virginia in a bony hug. Her earrings poked Virginia's neck; little chandeliers dangling almost down to her shoulders on stretched lobes. The pink stones in the earrings matched her bright lipstick, nearly the exact shade of her sandals and bag. She'd moved into Harbor Vale after selling her home to Belle-meade in the spring, but she looked so put together. Virginia wondered whether she needed assistance or just wanted the community that came with a place like that. A pang of jealousy flowed through her as she stepped back from Jan's arms and flashed her a strained smile.

The others arrived, and the group walked through the gardens, taking pictures and pointing out the flowers and groupings they wanted to feature. Minor squabbles arose —which areas deserved the front page, in what order the rest should follow—but Virginia hardly noticed them. She could only think of the ambush she'd faced at breakfast, Jan's vibrancy, and whether a life at Harbor Vale was really something to keep resisting. Maybe it could bring her some peace, some stability. If she'd even be allowed in if they found out she was a murder suspect.

When the group made it back to the pavilion where they'd left all their treats for the post-tour discussion, the talk turned from flowers to gossip. Who had moved, who had died, and who had opened themselves up to love and gone on a date.

But there was only one topic on Jan's mind. "So, Virginia, is it true? Was it really your nail file that killed that new Breeze Village guy?" Jan's voice carried across the pavilion. All eyes turned to Virginia, and she looked down at her sneakers as her cheeks flushed.

"I, well…" Virginia couldn't think of anything to say. She hadn't expected anyone in Seaview to know about that, but of course, word traveled fast.

"And you and he got into a screaming fight just days before the murder, right? I heard you're the prime suspect." Jan sounded like she'd never been more thrilled to have a scoop. Virginia swore she was speaking a little slower, annunciating a little more, making a performance of her questions.

Like the savior Virginia didn't think she deserved, Dorothea spoke up. "Virginia didn't kill that asshole. Rumor has it pretty much everyone hated him. Say, Virginia, are you going to solve this one, too?"

"I, err, what?"

"Like the other Breeze Village murders earlier this year. You solved those when no one else gave them a second thought. And now someone stole your nail file to kill this guy. Are you going to try to figure out who it was?" Dorothea looked at Virginia like it was the most obvious thing in the world.

Virginia stammered, all eyes on her. "I just want to cooperate with the police and make sure the killer is caught."

Jan laughed and Dorothea looked disappointed. For the first time, Virginia felt like she should involve herself. Like someone expected more from her than standing idly by, cooperating with the police whenever they had questions.

"I just… I mean, it's different. Before, those were people like us. And no one was taking it seriously. Russ, this guy, he's something else entirely. And the police are on it."

Dorothea frowned. "I just thought, since your name is associated with it, you'd be trying to figure out the truth."

All eyes were on Virginia. She could almost feel them, their gazes heating her skin.

Someone else piped up, "Are you still planning to move in there?"

Another voice, "Are they still taking new residents? With the new owner dead, some people are talking about the whole place shutting down."

The world around Virginia seemed to spin, the flowers beyond the pavilion blending with the bright colors of the Garden Review Society members, and her stomach rebelled against the cereal she had eaten earlier. "Excuse me," she mumbled. "I'm not feeling well."

She was halfway back to the parking lot before she felt she could breathe again. She chanced a nervous glance behind her. No one had followed her. She was alone. But though no one had come after her, their expectations lingered. *I just thought, since your name is associated with it, you'd be trying to figure out the truth.* Was that the expectation she'd set this spring? That she was some sort of investigator?

The thought scared and thrilled her. She didn't want their expectations, but she couldn't stop the pride from welling up at their belief in her.

NEITHER MARNEY nor Lawrence was available later that night, and neither Jack nor Stephanie knocked on

Virginia's door to talk more about the various options for her increasing need of assistance. She had the evening to herself, and she didn't want it.

When morning rolled around and her friends responded—Lawrence had a bowling match; Marney was meeting Dylan and had a doctor's appointment—she spent the day in the garden. It was Saturday, and Lucy was coming over for dinner that night. Virginia couldn't keep from looking at her watch every twenty minutes, just trying to make it through the day. She pulled her phone from her pocket every so often, unsure what she was hoping for. A distraction. Someone to ask her to go somewhere, to do something other than sit with her own thoughts.

The day came and went. Dinner passed quickly. Virginia knew Jack had told his sister about their ambush, about Virginia's response, and neither of them brought it up that evening. Though Virginia spent a week at Lucy's every now and then, the bulk of her time was spent at Jack's. The original plan to alternate weeks had been harder on everyone, and it was easier just to stay in one place. Since Jack and Stephanie had more room, that's where Virginia had settled in. She was their burden, and Lucy was aware and supportive but not bearing the brunt of it herself.

When Virginia excused herself to her room after dinner, she heard the three of them talking in low voices in the living room. She wanted to drown their voices out. She wanted to run back down the hall and scream at them, to tell them she was a whole person and not a problem to be discussed, to be dealt with. But as long as she was living in their house, she knew she was a burden.

Instead, she turned on the television Jack and Stephanie had dug out of their attic, old and chunky and in too good of condition to discard but too obsolete to keep in the house. They'd stuck it on top of the guest room dresser when it became clear Virginia would occupy that room. She cranked the volume up, a Hallmark movie blaring and masking the voices in the living room.

As she drifted to sleep, a pillow over her head muting the movie muting the voices, Virginia planned the events of the next day. She couldn't wait for this to resolve itself any longer. Couldn't wait for Michelle to come to her, saying, "Breeze Village is ready to welcome you!" Couldn't wait for the detective to get around to investigating Russ's emotionally distant wife, the woman calling his secret phone, the shady business partners he must have had. She knew that if she was going to stand a chance at moving things in the direction she wanted them to go, she needed to take ownership and get involved. Really get involved. Starting with talking to Michelle.

Virginia practiced the confrontation as she drove to Breeze Village. Even alone in her car, she struggled to sound convincing, but she felt ready by the time she pulled into the parking lot, already sweltering in the mid-morning heat.

Jane was knitting on the front porch, rocking back and forth in a rocking chair and humming as she worked. She smiled up at Virginia, but Virginia thought there was some pity, some hesitation in the smile. She forced her own lips to curl up as her cheeks flushed, and she hurried into the building.

The aromas of breakfast poured from the dining room out into the lobby, and Virginia's stomach grumbled as she signed in. She'd been so determined to get here and confront Michelle that she hadn't eaten breakfast.

Michelle wasn't working at the desk in the lobby, but Virginia heard voices coming from inside her old office. The office that had so briefly been Russ's. She wondered if Michelle had taken it back over.

The office door was cracked, pushed nearly closed but not latched, and the voices inside were arguing. Michelle was speaking firmly, her sentences short and clipped. The other voice was male, slightly nasal.

"What are you trying to do here?" the man asked. "It was completely irresponsible. How do you expect—"

Michelle cut him off, her voice raising now. "Enough."

Virginia took a deep breath and counted down from three. When she reached zero, she knocked at the door before she had a chance to convince herself otherwise. Her knock pushed the door slightly open, and she could see that the man arguing with Michelle was Liam. Curiosity arose about what would happen to Liam, Kim, and Russ's other new hires now that he was gone. Would Michelle keep them on? Was it her call to make?

"Can I help you?" Michelle's tone was curt. She didn't invite Virginia to step into the office.

Virginia made herself keep her chin up high even as her voice came out soft and meek. "I came to talk to you."

"I'm in the middle of something."

"It won't take long."

Michelle didn't nod or give her a signal to go on, but she didn't object further. Virginia looked between her and Liam, waiting for him to excuse himself, but he didn't.

Virginia opened her mouth, cleared her throat, and began the words she'd rehearsed on her drive over. "Michelle, I was on the waitlist here before Russ's ownership. I had an agreement with Breeze Village, not with you personally. An agreement I believe Russ was legally obligated to maintain. But seeing as he is no longer with us, and as you are General Manager, I wanted to address it with you."

The words sounded unnatural as they fell from her lips. Rehearsed, because they were. She saw a glint of something in Michelle's eyes. Could it have been pride? She wanted to believe she'd impressed Michelle by standing up for herself, but before Michelle could answer, Liam spoke up.

"We have to be careful who we let into this place. We don't want the reputation of Breeze Village to be tarnished any further." As he sneered those last words, he glared at Michelle.

"I'm sure your little politician girlfriend will still tolerate being associated with you even if you're linked to Breeze Village in its time of turmoil. And either way, that's not really my problem." Michelle shoved past Liam and Virginia and left without addressing Virginia's request.

Liam sneered at her and followed Michelle out, shutting the office door behind him and leaving Virginia standing alone in front of the closed door. Her jaw hung slightly open in surprise at being so dismissed.

She'd expected an argument. Expected a no. Expected to have to continue the fight. She hadn't expected to be dismissed as if she hadn't said anything at all.

Virginia wandered into the dining room. If her mission to make progress on her housing predicament had been unsuccessful, at least she could get a free breakfast out of it. She walked down the spread of food, fixing herself a plate of pancakes and eggs and pouring herself a coffee, then turned to survey the room. Ronald was sitting alone, eating his own breakfast. Virginia walked over and joined him.

After cursory greetings and a few bites of pancakes, Virginia couldn't hold it in any longer. "You really don't think I killed Russ?"

He cocked his head to the side, chewing his food. "No. I told you that already."

"Liam just basically called me a murderer to my face. Well, said I can't move in here because I'd tarnish the place's reputation."

"Don't listen to him. He was Russ's yes-man and now he's just trying to grab at any bit of power he can."

The words were a relief. Virginia sipped her coffee, considering them. They were a slight balm, but they didn't change the fact that her reputation preceded her. Jan and Dorothea and the rest of the Garden Review Society had already heard of her connection to the murder.

"I can't help but wonder how it was your nail file that killed him, though," Ronald said.

"You and me both."

"Are you going to try to solve this one like you did before?"

Virginia took another sip of coffee before responding. "I think I might have to."

Ronald turned and gave her a quizzical look.

"Even if not everyone thinks I did it, everyone looks at me and immediately thinks of the murder. Whether they think I'm a killer or not, it's not a great reputation. And I need a place to live."

"Liam can't actually keep you out of this place. He doesn't have the authority."

"But we don't know what's going to happen with this place now that Russ is gone. If Michelle will take it back over or what. And she didn't seem too keen on putting me back on the waitlist, either."

Ronald opened his mouth as if to respond but then closed it. Neither one spoke for a while, and Virginia wondered if they were both considering the same thing: whether Harbor Vale or someplace else would hold her reputation against her in the same way.

Finally, Ronald broke the silence. "Who do you think did it?"

Virginia looked at him, trying to decide how much to share. Only a few months ago, she thought he might have murdered someone. Now, though, she trusted him. So she shared what she knew.

"His wife seems off. Russ was definitely cheating, but I don't know if she knew. I talked with her briefly, and her only response to my condolences was to assure me that the business would survive. Not exactly the grieving widow I'd expected. Then there's Kim. She was sneaking around in Russ's room after she found him and just seemed more affected by his death than I'd expect."

Ronald weighed what Virginia had just told him, and she continued, "And who knows what kinds of enemies he may have made in his business."

"Have you thought about Michelle?"

Virginia nearly choked on her coffee. She waited for Ronald to elaborate.

"She sells the place for cash, then Russ dies, and she's basically in control again. Then there's her big announcement. Seems to me like she's positioning herself as a savior. She gets all the glory for uncovering this scheme and cleaning the place up." Ronald shrugged.

Virginia's mind whirled. "But she wasn't at the casino. She couldn't have done it."

Ronald gave another shrug. The elevator dinged and a small group poured out, loudly making their way into the dining room.

"Ronald!" one of them exclaimed. "How's about a game of cards?"

"At this hour?"

As the group neared, Virginia excused herself. Michelle, a suspect? It didn't fit, but as she returned to her car and headed back across town, she couldn't shake Ronald's words from her head.

Marney took Virginia up on the offer to share her recommendation for an eye doctor, then took her up on the offer to drive her. When Virginia picked her up, Marney was nervous, her fingers looping yarn around her crochet hook at lightning speed, her breathing slow and deliberate.

"You know," Marney said, halfway through the drive, "I kind of like having a chauffeur. Maybe I shouldn't get a new license."

"And when it rains again?"

"Lawrence will just have to quit his bowling league and give up on dating and drive us both around."

Virginia laughed. By the time she parked at the doctor's office, she thought Marney's mood had lightened, but as they stepped out of the car she could hear Marney's slow, deep breathing. In to a count of four, then out to a count of six. She shoved down the guilt she felt for her part in exacerbating her friend's anxiety.

The doctor's office was sleek and modern. Low carpet

in various shades of blue and gray met walls covered with textured wallpaper, metallic accents glinting in the bright light. Every surface gleamed. Even the magazines on the low table in the waiting area were in perfect condition, not a crumpled or ripped page in sight.

On the walls hung diagrams of the eye and prints of famous paintings, at odds with each other but all in pristine frames.

Marney walked to the front desk to check in and Virginia turned to take a seat.

"Well, I never!" The door from the hallway leading to the exam rooms opened and a familiar voice grabbed Virginia's attention. She looked up to see Jan walking toward her. "I was just in here for my exam and was thinking how I never see anybody I know out and about anymore, and now here you are!"

Jan paid her copay and, to Virginia's displeasure, returned to the waiting area and took a seat next to Virginia.

"I am just so sad I never get to see all my old neighborhood friends anymore. Ever since Bellemeade came through. Well, I really shouldn't talk bad about them, not after how much they paid me for my house, but I just miss our old get-togethers. And don't get me wrong, the garden club is great and all, but I don't just want to get together and talk about flowers. I want all the juicy gossip."

Of course she did.

Virginia put on her best smile. "It just isn't the same, is it? But I'm sure there are social activities at Harbor Vale."

Jan let out an exaggerated groan. "How many times do

I have to play bingo? Or do arts and crafts? No one there wants to just sit around and talk. It's either activities, or everyone's in their rooms with the doors shut."

Virginia looked up, grateful to see Marney making her way toward them.

"But enough about me," Jan said in a tone that made Virginia's stomach sink. "What are you up to these days? I heard about Dr. DiMarco closing down his practice. You must have nothing to do anymore. How are you keeping busy?"

Virginia hadn't even heard that Dr. DiMarco was closing his practice. He'd only told her he couldn't keep her on with so much uncertainty.

"I, err, I'm going to be working with Gemma more on the Garden Review. She's been trying to teach herself to bake. I might help her with that, too."

"You'd be doing us all a service if you do that! Those cupcakes!" Jan mimed gagging, and Marney let out a small giggle.

Jan continued, "One of my new neighbors has a kid who is all about volunteer work. I could introduce you. You know, in case you're looking for ways to bolster your reputation after that nasty business with the Breeze Village guy. What's his name, Rusty?"

"Russ," Virginia muttered.

"Russ, that's it!"

At that moment, a nurse opened the door and poked her head in. "Marney Richards?"

Marney stood, then looked back toward Virginia. "Will you come back with me?"

Virginia could have cried with relief as she bid Jan

goodbye and followed Marney and the nurse down the hall.

* * *

MARNEY'S new prescription would be ready in a week. When Virginia dropped her off at Breeze Village, Marney had sheepishly thanked her for coming back to the exam room with her and apologized for being so childishly nervous. Virginia hadn't been able to contain a belly laugh as she thanked Marney for saving her from any further conversation with Jan.

"She means well," Marney said, though she didn't sound entirely convinced.

"I would just rather she mean well in someone else's business, not mine."

Virginia watched Marney climb the steps to the main building and disappear inside. She weighed her options: go back to Jack's house and risk facing him or Stephanie, go to the beach, drive around town aimlessly, or... She couldn't think of anything else. She watched the building as she thought about how much smaller her life felt now than it ever had before, and then the previous day's conversation with Ronald played in her head.

A tiny voice piped up in the back of her mind. *You could investigate.* She shook her head, arguing with herself. Investigate what? *Michelle. Kim. Poke around in Russ's office.* It didn't feel like a good idea. It felt like something she would later have to explain to her kids or to a policeman while watching them look at her like she was an idiot.

But it also seemed like a better option than anything else she could come up with.

Music drifted from one of the activities rooms into the lobby. Someone was playing the piano and voices were singing along, some closer to the melody than others. She checked in at the front desk, then stood in the lobby, regretting her decision. She had no idea where Michelle was, and she stood no chance of getting into the office to poke around during the day.

She poured herself a glass of iced tea in the dining room and started toward the elevator. She hadn't had a chance to ask Colleen about any of her theories, and now seemed like as good a time as any. The elevator doors opened, and Virginia started as Kim walked out, arms full of linens.

"Good afternoon." Kim looked good. Healthy. Happy, even. No sign of the swollen eyes or the distant expression she'd had immediately following Russ's death.

"Err, hi. Do you know where Michelle is, by any chance?"

"She's out today." Kim turned and resumed walking, but Virginia called her back.

"You look good. I'm happy to see it."

Kim looked her up and down, considering her response. In the end, she said, "Thanks. I'm sorry for being a jerk to you before. If you did kill that asshole, thank you."

Virginia's mouth fell open in surprise.

Kim chuckled. "He was a two-timing piece of shit. I mean, I wish I hadn't been the one to find him." Her eyes clouded over for a moment, and Virginia knew where she was in her mind. Knew how hard it was to stop seeing the scene over and over. But Kim shook her head slightly and continued. "But I'm glad he's dead."

Virginia continued to stand in silence, no clue how to respond.

"We were dating," Kim volunteered. She gestured with her head for Virginia to follow her as she took up walking toward the laundry room at the far end of the long hallway lined with doors. It was in this hallway that Virginia had found Ruth, then later Genie and Byron. She couldn't help but shudder.

They reached the end of the hall, and Kim hadn't said anything further. Impatient, Virginia prompted her, "So, you and Russ?"

Kim nodded. "He was dating a bunch of people."

"Did you see him that night? The night he…"

Kim shook her head. Her mouth tugged down into a slight frown. "I was under strict instructions not to go to his room. He was always like that, so secretive. He made the rules, always. We never went to his place, only mine. He was supposed to come to my room that night, but he didn't."

"What did you do?"

"I went pounding on his door, instructions be damned. I was so mad. The door was locked, of course, and he didn't answer. I gave up, and I was ready to ignore him at breakfast, give him the silent treatment. But then he didn't show up, and I went to go pound on his door some more. Only that time, it wasn't closed all the way. And that's when I…"

Kim shuddered, and Virginia shifted her weight from one foot to the other, unsure what to say.

"Anyway," Kim said, jerking her chin up and setting her jaw. "Serves him right."

When Kim yanked open the door of the large washing machine and began shoving sheets inside, Virginia mumbled a goodbye and hurried down the hall. She wasn't sure what to make of Kim's admissions, her sudden desire to share.

Twenty minutes later, she'd knocked on Colleen's door, to no response, and paid Gemma a visit in her cottage. She hadn't seen Colleen, either, but she'd been busy making cinnamon buns all morning. Gemma offered one to Virginia, who choked down a bite and gave an enthusiastic, if not truthful, thumbs up.

By the time she was making her way back through the courtyard and into the main building on her way to her car, Virginia felt as deflated as one of Gemma's bakes. She appreciated Kim's information, but she already knew that Russ was sleeping around and Kim had been the one to find him. None of the information was especially helpful, and without Michelle or Colleen around, Virginia felt stalled.

She crossed the lobby to turn in her visitor's badge. The receptionist was away from her desk so Virginia set the badge on top and signed herself out on the clipboard, then started toward the door. Two steps in, she stopped, then spun around. The receptionist was gone. Now was her chance.

Virginia hurried across the lobby, cringing as her

sneakers squeaked on the linoleum. She reached the office door and grabbed the handle. Locked.

She let out the breath she hadn't realized she'd been holding. Defeated, she turned back to the door. The sound of her own breathing filled her ears, and she wondered if it was truly as loud as it seemed or if it was just the adrenaline. She couldn't slow her heart rate. She padded over to Michelle's desk, gripping the dark wood to steady herself, then looked down.

Hastily, constantly looking around to see if anyone was coming, Virginia jiggled the drawers on the desk. The first was locked. The next contained hand sanitizer, a mini pack of tissues, and a bag of trail mix. Not the exciting find Virginia was hoping for. She gripped the handle on the last drawer and tugged. Nothing. Frustrated, she gave it a harder tug and was surprised when it sprung open. Sitting in the drawer was a heap of manilla folders.

Virginia grabbed the first one and flicked through the contents. Visitor logs, showing the names of all recent visitors and their dates and times of visitation. Her own name was among the most frequent on the sheet.

In the distance a door shut, and Virginia quickened her pace, flipping through the next few folders. Nothing jumped out as suspicious, and as footsteps sounded in the hall, she shoved them all back into the drawer and slammed it shut. The drawer stuck halfway closed, and panic rose in Virginia as she frantically jiggled the drawer, trying to get it to shut. Finally, the drawer slid closed just before the footsteps rounded the corner from the hallway into the lobby.

Virginia turned to see who it was and noticed a small yellow sticky note on the floor as she turned.

"Can I help you?" The receptionist was back.

"I just dropped this and was trying to pick it up." Virginia bent to pick up the note, her groans and struggle to bend down to the floor entirely truthful.

The receptionist looked her up and down, mouth pulled back in a suspicious frown. "Did you sign out already?"

Virginia nodded. Her fingers wrapped around the little piece of paper and she stood, hurrying to the door as quickly as she could. It wasn't until she was in her car alone that she looked down at the paper in her hand. In tight, neat handwriting was written *Cindy, 2 p.m.*

* * *

IT WAS all Virginia could do not to turn right around and pay Marney a visit to see what she made of the note. She fought the internal battle with herself, not wanting to bring Marney deeper into this but desperately wanting her opinion. She considered going to talk with Ronald but wasn't ready to open up to him with new information yet. Instead, she drove home, hands shaking, as excitement built inside her. She had a next step: pay Cindy a visit.

Through dinner and Jeopardy and getting ready for bed, Virginia's mind was on Russ's wife. But the excitement was tempered by reality as she faced a familiar problem: She had a suspect but didn't know where to find them. Virginia thought back to earlier in the year, her multiple attempts to get Matt's address before Marney ultimately snagged it for her. She couldn't ask Marney to get involved, and she wasn't sure Marney would be able to find Cindy's address anyway.

Even so, by early afternoon the next day she found herself at Breeze Village, knocking at the door to Gemma's cottage.

"Come in!"

Virginia let herself in and found Gemma sprawled on her couch, face covered in what looked like pale cloth with holes cut out for the eyes, nose, and mouth.

"What's wrong with your face?"

"It's a beauty mask. It hydrates my skin so I can stay youthful."

In that mask, Gemma looked more like a serial killer than anything else, but Virginia took a seat without mentioning it.

"What brings you here?" Gemma asked. A wry smile suggested she knew Virginia had come with a request and she was open to hearing it.

"I had another suggestion for a garden we could review." She hesitated.

"Oh, yeah?" Gemma prompted.

"I was thinking... I was thinking we could pay Russ's wife a visit. I've heard she gardens and thought it might also be a bit of a tribute to Russ."

Gemma's face darkened. "I am not turning my legitimate magazine into a front for your private investigative business. And I am certainly not making any tribute to that asshole, even if it's fake."

Virginia immediately regretted her request and felt a trace of relief at the rejection. She had completely fabricated the fact that Cindy gardened. If Gemma had agreed and they'd gone and discovered a tiny, ratty garden, or worse, no garden at all… Virginia shuddered. Getting Cindy's address wasn't worth humiliating her friend.

She opened her mouth to apologize, but another knock at the door interrupted her. Without waiting for a response, Colleen pulled the door open and stumbled inside. Her eyes widened in surprise when she saw that Virginia was there, and she looked from her to Gemma and back, feeling out the tension in the room. Then she let out a giggle and tried to stifle it, which only made her laugh harder.

"I'm sorry, I didn't mean to interrupt," Colleen said in between her laughter. "And what's that on your face?"

Gemma's frown lifted and Virginia relaxed her shoulders. "You're not interrupting," Gemma said. "We were just finishing up."

"Actually," Virginia said, turning to Colleen, "you might be able to help."

Colleen cocked her head to the side. "How's that?"

"I'm trying to locate someone. I might have something of theirs if that helps." She thought of the hotel key from out west and wondered if Cindy had touched it, if it had been a trip they'd taken together, or if she'd even known he'd gone.

But Colleen frowned and shook her head. "I'm afraid I can't help. My visions have been… hazy lately."

Colleen turned her attention toward the television where Gemma was watching reality TV, pointedly ending the conversation there. Virginia wanted to press harder, but Gemma cut her a look, and she knew the conversation was over. She'd need to find Cindy's address through other means.

Frustrated, Virginia made her way to the dining room, and when she found Ronald, Patricia, and a small group of other residents playing poker, she asked to join them. She didn't know whether she'd tell Ronald about the sticky note—certainly not in front of other people—but the companionship alone was soothing, and she thought someone there might be able to help.

"Do any of you know where Russ lives? Well, lived, I guess," she asked the group. They all looked at her, a few with raised eyebrows, and she said, "I want to send flowers to his wife."

Ronald grinned as wide as she'd ever seen. He knew she wasn't sending her flowers. She was investigating.

Patricia chimed in, "I do. I saw it on a form in his office when I was there filling out paperwork when I moved in. I have a photographic memory."

Patricia recited the address, and Virginia asked her to slow down, then repeat it once Virginia had pulled a pen and notepad from her purse. It was all she could do not to run out of Breeze Village and straight to Cindy's house. She lost the next three poker games before finally leaving as nonchalantly as she could.

As she stood from the table, Ronald gave her a wink, and she couldn't disguise the spring in her step as she walked at her best approximation of a normal pace out to her car.

CHAPTER 10

Virginia's bi-weekly lunch with Marney and Lawrence had been one of the highlights of her life recently, and she usually spent the two weeks between lunches looking forward to the next. Especially since Lawrence had been busy looking for love and Marney had been spending more and more time preparing for the launch of her crochet shop, their lunches had been one of the few times they were all reliably available. This week, however, Virginia would have forgotten the lunch entirely had Lawrence not texted to tell them he'd be late.

She'd spent the night tossing and turning, thinking of how she'd approach Cindy. When sleep found her, she dreamed that she arrived at Cindy's house and Russ was there, zombified and looking for revenge. He'd stabbed her with her own nail file while she protested that she hadn't been the one to murder him until she woke, drenched in sweat and panting.

Over her third cup of coffee, Virginia thought she'd

come up with a plan to approach Cindy without arousing suspicion. As she was dressing for her investigative adventure, her phone chimed with Lawrence's text. As soon as lunch was over, she promised herself, she'd go.

Virginia picked up Marney, still not road legal until her new prescription arrived and she re-took her test, and they met Lawrence at Miss B's.

The fatty smell of fried chicken and the sound of oil popping in heavy cast iron greeted them as they entered the packed restaurant. The heat of the mass of bodies challenged the air conditioning, and when a waitress approached their table, sweat was beaded on her forehead.

"What can I get y'all started with?" She flashed a broad smile and wiped a piece of hair from her face.

"Three sweet teas, please," Lawrence said, returning her smile, "and can we start with the fried pickles?"

Virginia crinkled her nose. She'd never grown to like pickles, though Lawrence and Marney devoured them every time they visited Miss B's.

Marney asked Lawrence about a recent bowling tournament and a date he'd been on that Virginia hadn't known about. She felt a twinge of hurt that Marney knew what was going on in Lawrence's life so much more than she did, but then as he spoke, she found her mind drifting to Cindy again. She kept picturing the sticky note with Cindy's name on it, wondering how Michelle and Cindy were connected, whether they could have had anything to do with Russ's murder.

"Earth to Virginia." Lawrence was looking across the table at her, eyebrows raised in bemusement.

"Are you that anxious to get back to Jack's house?" Marney teased.

Virginia mumbled an apology.

"How has it been since the bingo tournament?" Marney asked. Not *since Russ's murder,* Virginia noticed.

"Jack is pretty much as expected. Apoplectic that I somehow got myself involved in another murder case. Stephanie's even more on edge than expected. She can't handle the littlest bit of stress lately. It's driving me crazy."

"Does she have a gallery show coming up?"

Virginia couldn't remember. She was debating whether to admit she'd either forgotten or never asked her daughter-in-law what was going on in her life or to lie and say there was definitely no gallery show. Before she had to make a decision, the waitress returned with their plates. Perfect timing.

As they dug into their meals, Virginia's phone chimed again. A reminder flashed across the screen. *Work tomorrow 12 p.m.* Her stomach dropped.

Lawrence saw the words flash across the screen and noticed Virginia's frown. "I heard about Dr. DiMarco."

Virginia squirmed under his sympathetic gaze.

Marney caught her eyes and piped up, "Lawrence, I might need your eye for design for my website. Someone at Breeze Village says she used to do web design, but I'm not convinced she can actually see anymore, and I know I can't do it myself."

Virginia and Marney exchanged a small smile. Virginia was grateful her friend had stepped in to change the topic of conversation, and she sipped her tea and thought about visiting Cindy and tried to look like she was listening to Marney and Lawrence talk.

As they were scraping the last bites off their plates, Lawrence looked at his watch and announced that he had to leave. "I've got a bowling match."

Virginia nodded, but Marney narrowed her eyes and gave him a skeptical look. "It's Thursday. You don't bowl on Thursdays."

Virginia perked up.

Lawrence sighed. "I've got a date. But I didn't want to tell you in case it didn't go well."

"We won't badger you about it," Virginia said, beaming.

"Liar," Lawrence said, grinning right back. "If I make it to evening and don't have a text from each of you asking how the date went, I'll call Dylan and have her send out her officers to check if you've dropped dead. And I didn't want to have to describe another bad date if that's how it goes."

Marney squeezed Lawrence's hand. "Then let's hope it's not another bad date."

She and Virginia both kissed Lawrence on the cheek, and he took off toward his car. Virginia had to consciously slow her walk as she and Marney made their way to her own car. She was so close to being able to pay Cindy a visit, and every nerve in her body was shaking with anticipation. Marney was scarcely out of the car when Virginia peeled off, unable even to sit there until her friend was all the way into the building.

Heart racing, Virginia drove toward Cindy's house.

* * *

"Hɪ, I found this at Breeze Village and I think it might have belonged to your husband." Virginia practiced her greeting in the car, voice shaking every time. In the glove compartment was a silver watch, slightly battered but well-maintained, ticking away. When she'd pulled it from the safe that morning, one of the few objects she'd brought with her to Jack's house instead of storing it in the storage unit with the rest of her belongings, her heart had thudded in her chest.

This is wrong.

She'd shaken her head and banished the thought. *It's the only way. I need her to talk to me.*

Of course, it wasn't the only way; Virginia might have pretended to be selling makeup or fundraising door to door, or simply pretended she'd gotten a friend's address wrong. But she wanted—needed—Cindy to talk with her about Russ, and this was the best plan she could come up with as her brain whirred with excitement, moving too quickly to cling to any one idea.

As she drew nearer to the block where she knew Cindy lived, where Russ had lived, she tried not to picture Earl's face when she'd given him that watch for one of their first Christmases together. Tried not to picture his face if he knew she was using it as a tool in this investigation.

If she told him the stakes, she knew he'd have torn the watch from his own wrist and insisted she do whatever she had to in order to clear her name, save her reputation, and secure housing for herself. But she knew it would break his heart anyway.

Virginia rounded the corner onto Cindy's street and counted the house numbers until she came to the one Patricia had assured her was correct. When she got to Cindy's house, she couldn't help but let out a low chuckle. The small garden that wrapped from the front of the house around the side was gorgeous. She pulled out her phone and snapped a picture to show Gemma.

She gripped the watch in her hand, the band dangling such that the cool metal brushed the back of her hand and the top of her wrist. The paved walkway from the street to the front porch was cracked, the roots from several mature oaks poking up and creating rifts in the concrete. Virginia stepped gingerly, careful not to trip, and gripped the wooden railing as she climbed the steps up to the front door.

The door was painted a deep brown, and a golden lion with a ring in its mouth hung from the center. Gorgeous, if unoriginal. Virginia gripped the door knocker and rapped three times. *Whap! Whap! Whap!*

Nothing.

The curtains were drawn in every window on the front of the house, so Virginia couldn't tell whether someone were moving about inside. She raised her hand to try again, but footsteps inside interrupted her. She could hear a muffled voice behind the door, growing louder as the footsteps drew nearer.

The door swung open just enough to reveal Cindy's head as she leaned outside. She was holding her phone up to her ear and frowning. Her frown deepened when she saw Virginia.

"Can I help you?"

Virginia cleared her throat, choking slightly as Cindy's heavy perfume drifted through the barely-open doorway. She wondered how Russ could live there and not reek of the stuff. She held up the watch, reciting the words she'd practiced earlier. "I found this at Breeze Village and I think it may have belonged to your husband."

If it were possible, Cindy's frown deepened further. Her eyes lingered on the watch for only a second, her nose crinkling up slightly, before her gaze returned to Virginia. "No, that's not his."

"Are… Are you sure?" Virginia stammered. She hadn't thought this far into the conversation.

"Russ would never wear something that looked like *that.*" The disdain in her voice made Virginia flinch.

"Anything to do with Russ," Cindy went on, "you can just take directly to the police."

Her meaning was clear. *I'm not going to talk about my husband.* Great.

Cindy continued to stand in the doorway, completely blocking Virginia's view inside.

"If we're done here…" Cindy didn't bother to finish the sentence before she turned away, slamming the door shut behind her.

Virginia could hear her resuming her phone conversation on the other side of the door, her voice raised, but she couldn't make out what she was saying. She cursed herself for her insistence that she didn't need hearing aids and unabashedly leaned her body against the door, pressing her ear to the wood as she strained to hear what Cindy was saying on the other side. She was definitely yelling, Virginia could tell, but that was all she could make out.

Virginia turned to leave and was halfway down the stairs when the door behind her swung open and Cindy came rushing out. "I'll be there tomorrow to—oh!" Her hand flew to her chest in surprise at the sight of Virginia. "You're still here."

Virginia apologized and took the stairs extra slowly, exaggerating the struggle to make it seem like she was just slow and hadn't been lingering on the porch trying to eavesdrop. Cindy stood at the top of the steps, eyes narrowed, and watched Virginia take the stairs and then carefully step across the uneven walkway toward the street. Virginia lowered herself into her car, not needing to exaggerate the difficulty there. One hand gripped the handle above the door as she eased herself in. With the car door still open, she heard Cindy resume her conversation, voice lowered.

"Sorry, someone was here. I'll see you tomorrow at six."

Virginia closed her car door and turned to take one more glance at Cindy, still standing atop the front stairs, arms folded across her chest. She kept her eyes narrowed and watched Virginia start the car and pull away.

AS SHE DROVE AWAY, Virginia considered how much it seemed that Cindy didn't want Virginia—or maybe anyone—to see inside her house. And if Cindy didn't want her to see inside, Virginia decided that was exactly what she should do next.

The drive back to Jack's and Stephanie's house was an internal battle.

You don't like strangers snooping around your house, either. Or you didn't, back when you had a house of your own.

But Cindy was being shady about it!

Shady, or just a woman who has twice now been harassed by you about her recently deceased husband and is getting tired of it?

Shady, for sure. And even if she wasn't, that was Russ's home, too. What might he have hidden in there?

By the time she'd pulled into the driveway, Virginia had fully made up her mind to go back there. Her thoughts kept going back to the phones hidden in a hollowed-out book in Russ's hotel room, and she told herself there was a good chance she could uncover a clue in his home that might give her a lead into who might have wanted him dead.

She went back the next evening, pulling up to the house at ten minutes after six and praying that wherever Cindy had gone to meet the person she'd been on the phone with the day before, she'd be there for a while. The sun was only just beginning to set, a long summertime evening still stretching before the town, and Virginia wished she had the cover of darkness for this.

She first walked right up to the front door and jiggled the handle. It was locked, as she'd expected. She looked to the two windows at the front of the house, curtains still drawn to conceal the rooms behind them, but decided against trying those. Even if one was unlocked, if she was going to try to enter via a window, she figured it shouldn't be in full view of the entire street.

Virginia made her way around the side of the house, sticking first to the side where tall bushes shielded it from the neighboring home. She approached one of the windows, placing the heels of her palms on the panes of glass and trying to slide them upward. No luck.

When the back door was just as secured as all the other points of entry, Virginia dug into the bottom of her purse for a safety pin, bent it, and shoved it into the lock like she knew what she was doing. After three minutes of franticly wiggling the pin around in the lock, she had to admit that she had no idea what she was doing and needed to find a different approach.

She eyed the back windows. On one side of the door were two small windows, but on the other side was a large bay window. It was quite high off the ground, but at least Virginia knew she'd be able to fit through it. Before she could talk herself out of it, Virginia grabbed a small landscaping rock from Cindy's garden and threw it as hard as she could muster at the window.

The shatter of the glass made Virginia jump. She looked around, eyes wide, panicking for the first time. She wanted to kick herself for coming here. What was she thinking?

She began to back away from the window, still looking around her frantically, waiting for a neighbor to pop out of their house and call her out. But no one came, and as she started to round the corner back to the front of the house, she stopped. She'd already broken the window.

Cindy was going to know someone was there. Virginia decided she might as well go inside.

She returned to the rear of the house and approached the shattered window. Jagged pieces of glass jutted into the opening, threatening to shred her upon entry. She grabbed a stick and began to stab at the glass, further breaking it to expand the opening until she felt certain she could fit through it.

Even with the window busted wide open, standing up close, Virginia knew she couldn't hoist herself up high enough to climb inside. She looked around for anything she might convert into makeshift stairs. The yard and back porch were devoid of any bench or patio furniture. But then Virginia's eyes landed on the plant stands framing the back door.

Her heart pounded in her ears, and she kept pausing to slow her breathing and listen for anyone who might be coming. Still no one came, and one by one, she removed the pots from the plant stands until she had two empty ones. They were metal, each with three little platforms for a potted plant. Almost like a tiny stepstool. A tiny stepstool not meant to support the weight of a human, she thought as she carried the stands over to the broken window.

Virginia leaned in and pushed back the curtains on the inside of the window. The window opened onto a kitchen, but there was no bench or furniture on the other side to shorten the step down. She leaned the two plant stands up against the brick wall of the house and stood there preparing to climb up onto them. If they collapsed and she fell, she'd fall into the busted window, gashing herself on the broken glass.

She did it anyway.

Virginia lifted one foot onto the lowest platform of one of the stands, the other foot still firmly planted on the ground. Ever so slowly she leaned forward, placing more and more weight on the plant stand. It held.

Finally, she took a deep breath and lifted the toes of her other foot off the ground. The plant stand was supporting her weight. She moved her second foot to the lowest platform of the second stand, then lifted her first foot onto the second platform of its stand, climbing them like stairs. When she had each foot on the tallest platform of the stands, it was only a few inches to step up to the windowsill. And a few feet down on the other side.

Virginia stood there for what might have been two or twenty minutes, considering what came next. Then she gripped the curtain hanging inside the window with both hands, gave it a tug to test the strength of the curtain rod, and stepped up.

One foot planted on the sill of the broken window. The other followed, her grip on the curtain the only thing steadying Virginia, and then she jumped down, the curtain rod supporting her just enough to slow her descent before it came crashing down on top of her.

Virginia stumbled forward, arms out in front of her to catch herself. Just as the voice in her head reminded her that this was exactly how you break an arm or a wrist, she stumbled into the kitchen table and caught herself before going all the way down. Her shoulder ached from where the curtain rod hit it, and she bashed her shin into one of the dining chairs. She knew it would bruise later, knew it would leave her entire shin purple and that she'd have to put away her capris in favor of long pants until it healed or Jack would kill her.

But she was inside.

Hardly able to believe it, Virginia looked around her, fumbling for a light. The kitchen was sleek and modern. The silver face of the refrigerator was entirely bare, without a family photo, birthday card, or wedding invitation in sight. There were no magnets on the fridge with which to secure any of those sentimental items if Russ or Cindy ever wanted to. It was a gorgeous, entirely impersonal room, like she'd walked into a model kitchen in a home improvement store.

The living room was equally lovely and equally bare of personal touches. A huge canvas hung over the couch with blocks of color reminiscent of a Rothko. Virginia pulled open the tiny drawers on the sleek black end tables. Both were completely empty.

She continued through the house, opening closet doors, checking inside drawers. Everything seemed entirely in order, nothing suspicious to be found. She made her way to the final room at the end of the hallway, a study. Black shelves lined gray walls, and a huge black desk occupied the center of the room. Maroon curtains covered the window in this room as they did the rest of the windows in the house.

Virginia approached the desk. In contrast to every other surface in the home, this one had papers on it. Manila folders filled neat filing stands, but several documents were spread on the desk like Cindy hadn't gotten around to putting them away yet. Virginia crept closer and leaned over, picking up one of the pages and holding it close to her face to make out what it said.

In block letters across the top of the page, it said *Letter of Intention to Offer*. Virginia's brows knit together as she continued to scan the page, trying to understand what she was holding. There was a name at the top of the letter that sounded familiar, though Virginia couldn't place it. *Hashim Odeh*. She scanned the paragraphs, then scanned them again. It was an offer to buy Breeze Village.

She set the page down and picked up another. It looked nearly identical, but this time she knew the name at the top of the offer letter. *Michelle Martin*.

Virginia looked the letter over again. Was she wrong and this was the offer letter Russ and Cindy put in when they bought the place from Michelle? But the buyer was definitely Michelle, and the date was only a week before, mere days after Russ had been killed.

Virginia dropped the paper like it burned her fingertips, staggering back slightly. And before she could fully wrap her mind around what she'd just discovered, a sound caught her attention. The unmistakable sound of the front door opening.

Virginia froze. Her panicked breathing was ragged, and she tried to slow it so she could hear the sounds of Cindy moving through the home.

"Shit!" she cursed, realizing she'd left lights on throughout the house and her car parked right out front. "Shit!"

Virginia whirled around, looking for an escape.

"Hello?" Cindy's voice echoed through the house. It wavered. She was scared, Virginia realized.

For a moment, Virginia felt relieved. If Cindy was frightened, that meant she didn't immediately know who was in her home. Her immediate reaction hadn't been to storm in, fury raining down on Virginia. But as soon as the relief bubbled up inside her, guilt sliced through it. More than the damage she'd caused in the kitchen, Virginia knew the fear Cindy was feeling and hated to be the reason for it.

"Is anyone there?"

Virginia couldn't hear Cindy's footsteps as she crept

through the house. She stood stock-still, listening intently, sure she was seconds away from being caught. Then a small scream came from the other end of the house, and Virginia knew Cindy had made it to the kitchen and found the busted window and curtain rod ripped from the wall.

The front door lay between the study and the kitchen. The living room separated the kitchen from the entryway, while on Virginia's side, the long hallway fed into the foyer. If Cindy was in the kitchen, the front door wasn't visible to her. Virginia could make a run for it.

Still, Virginia waited. As each second ticked by, she knew Cindy might be closer to finishing her examination of the kitchen, closer to making her way to the other end of the house where Virginia stood frozen. But she couldn't bring herself to move.

A door squeaked open, and Virginia knew Cindy had gone out back to check for signs of the intruder. Now was her chance.

She counted down from three in her head, taking off at zero without giving herself any more time to consider her chances for success. She padded as quickly and as quietly as she could down the hallway.

She passed a bedroom. Then a bathroom. Another bedroom. The entryway was so close.

The back door slammed shut, and Cindy's footsteps were heading toward her. Virginia picked up her pace, and her sneaker squeaked on the wood floor.

"Who's there?" Cindy's voice sounded more aggressive now, and Virginia's stomach turned as she crossed the last few feet to the door.

Virginia gripped the door handle and slipped outside as quickly as she could, then pulled the door closed behind her. She held the handle turned in her hand, keeping the latch released to avoid a sound as she shut the door. On the other side, she could hear Cindy pass through the entryway and down the hall, still yelling to see who was there.

She let out the breath she hadn't realized she'd been holding.

She'd made it out.

Darkness was beginning to fall, and Virginia stumbled once as she hurried down the cracked concrete walkway to her car, recovering her balance before she went down. She grabbed at the handle to the car door and in her haste, her fingers slipped off. She cursed as she grabbed at it again, this time yanking the door open and throwing herself into the car as quickly as she could.

Why didn't I decide to become a stupid amateur detective slash criminal when I still had both my original knees and my back didn't hate me?

Virginia slammed the door shut and turned the key in the ignition at the same moment, pressing down on the gas and taking off into the night before she'd buckled her seatbelt. She turned off the street as soon as possible, then zigzagged through the neighborhood for five minutes before she pulled over and stopped.

Her chest heaved, and a cry escaped her. As the sun dipped fully below the horizon and darkness engulfed the neighborhood, Virginia lay her forehead on the steering wheel and shook with deep, wracking sobs.

* * *

WHEN SHE'D RECOVERED ENOUGH to drive again, Virginia pulled out her phone and typed out a message to Marney and Lawrence. *EMERGENCY. MEET AT LAWRENCE'S CONDO.* She pulled away from the curb, turned off her flashing hazard lights, and started toward Lawrence's beachside condo building.

She'd visited Lawrence twice since he moved: once for a small housewarming get-together and once when she'd driven to one of his bowling matches and a storm rolled in so Lawrence took her to his condo and then back to get her car when the storm subsided. She generally preferred to visit Marney at Breeze Village or to meet her friends out somewhere, but at the moment, she felt too fragile to be anywhere connected with Russ and Cindy.

Shortly after she'd resumed her drive, she heard sirens in the distance. Virginia continued putting distance between herself and Cindy's house, and the sirens grew louder. Moments later, two police cars whizzed past her in a blur of lights and sirens, and Virginia clenched the wheel so tight her knuckles went white as she tried to keep from shaking uncontrollably.

Her phone rang three times before Virginia made it to Lawrence's condo. One call from Marney and two from Lawrence. It wasn't until she was pulling into a visitor's spot in his complex's parking lot that she remembered Marney didn't have her new glasses yet. She bit back more tears as guilt piled on top of more guilt.

"Virginia, are you okay?" Lawrence pulled the door open at the first light knock and immediately wrapped

Virginia in his arms and pulled her inside. She leaned into his embrace, allowing him to fold her into himself as she surrendered to her sobs and shook.

"What happened?" When Lawrence pulled away from the hug he held Virginia in front of him, one big hand on each of her shoulders, and looked intently at her face.

"I... I... " Virginia choked on the words as she tried to get them out. Before she could collect herself enough to say anything, Marney came flying into the room without knocking. She was wrapped in a sparkling shawl, and it flowed behind her as she hurried inside and wrapped herself around Virginia.

"What happened?" Her concern echoed Lawrence's, and Virginia looked back and forth between her two friends, trying to find the words.

"I went to Cindy's house."

Both of her friends looked at her like she'd sprouted a second head.

"You what?" Marney asked sharply.

"Why?" Lawrence demanded.

Anger underlied both of their short responses, and Virginia wished she could dissolve on the spot.

"I'm sorry," she cried. "I'm so, so sorry. It was stupid!"

Marney's gaze remained cold, but Lawrence softened slightly and put one of his hands on the center of Virginia's back, rubbing small circles to soothe her slightly.

"Why don't we all go into the living room, and you can tell us what happened?" Lawrence guided Virginia to the couch with his hand on her back. Marney followed and took a seat opposite the room from Virginia and Lawrence.

"I went to Cindy's house," Virginia repeated. She took a deep breath and steadied herself before continuing. "I went to talk with her yesterday after our lunch, and she was acting so suspicious, and then she said over the phone she'd be somewhere at six today, so I thought—" Another sob racked her body and cut her off.

Virginia waited for one of her friends to say something, but neither did. They just looked at her, Marney's face cold, Lawrence's face more tender, and waited for her to go on.

"I broke in to try to see what she might be hiding, or what Russ might have been hiding before he died."

At this, both Lawrence's and Marney's eyes went wide with shock.

"You what?" they said in unison.

"I can't believe you," Marney added.

"Michelle was trying to buy back Breeze Village. I found the offer letter." If it were possible for Marney's eyes to grow wider, they did. Lawrence's brows knit together with confusion. Virginia went on, "And a second one. From Hashim Odeh?"

Marney sucked in a breath. "He owns Harbor Vale."

The three sat in stunned silence for a moment before Lawrence cleared his throat.

"Just to clarify, you weren't caught and arrested or injured or anything like that? The emergency was that you committed a premeditated crime?" There was a harder edge underneath his voice that Virginia hadn't expected. She looked up at his face in surprise. "I think we need to have a talk about texting etiquette and what constitutes an emergency."

Marney nodded. "That reminds me, I'm going to need a ride home. I drove here without a license, and I'm half blind until I get my new glasses."

Virginia grimaced and muttered an apology.

"But that's really curious," Marney continued. She met Virginia's eyes, and Virginia saw a glint of compassion and understanding that nearly made her burst into tears once again. "You should call Dylan."

"And say what? That I broke into someone's home and discovered no illegal activity by anyone besides myself?"

"Michelle just sold Breeze Village. Then she went on the news exposing a scandal there, and now she's trying to buy it back? What's her angle, devalue the place so she can make out with the business and a profit?"

"It's worth bringing to the police," Lawrence agreed.

Virginia considered it. She didn't trust Michelle, and she wanted the police to have every piece of information so they could identify the killer and strike Virginia from the suspect list as soon as possible. But she couldn't see a way to bring this information to the authorities without landing herself in worse trouble than she was already in.

"What happens to Breeze Village if Michelle is involved in something dodgy and gets put away?" Virginia wondered. "And if Hashim is mixed up in it, too? Where's an elderly person in Seaview supposed to go?"

Marney's lips pulled taut. "You have to tell the police. Virginia, look at me."

Virginia met her stare.

"You're not equipped to solve this thing. Plus, it's

dangerous. Bring the information to the professionals and let them do their jobs."

Virginia nodded, lowering her gaze to the floor. She knew Marney was right.

"When were the offer letters from? They were recent?" Lawrence asked.

Virginia nodded and opened her mouth to respond, then furrowed her brow and closed it again. "I can't remember. I know I checked. I'm sure they were recent." Her cheeks flushed. Here she was, resisting revealing her discovery to the police when she couldn't even remember it all herself.

By the time Virginia was climbing into her car, Marney silent in the passenger seat, she felt that calm exhaustion that follows a good cry. She was still sick to her stomach with guilt over the damage she'd done to Cindy's house, the violation of the security of her home that might leave Cindy uneasy for months, but breathing steadier than she was when she arrived an hour earlier.

"Are you going to call Dylan?" Marney's face was turned to the window and she didn't look at Virginia as she asked the question. Her voice was flat and resigned, like she expected Virginia to say no.

"Yes." The word tumbled quietly from Virginia's mouth, and Marney looked over at her and raised an eyebrow. "But I need a little time."

Marney sighed with frustration and went back to looking out the window into the darkness.

"I want to talk to Colleen first," Virginia said.

"Colleen's not going to be any help."

"Why not?"

Marney shrugged. "She just spends all her time in the garden, with Gemma, or in her room with her door closed. She stopped doing readings and hasn't mentioned a vision in weeks. The other day someone was asking her about lottery numbers, and instead of her usual scolding about not using her powers for vapid things like that, she mumbled something about severing her connection to the spirit world."

Virginia's brows knit together. Colleen had certainly been hard to find and unhelpful lately, but that was so unlike her. In the past, she'd flaunted her abilities, prophesying whether people wanted her guidance or not.

When Marney eased herself out of the car, she didn't say anything, just gave Virginia a long and meaningful glance before turning and making her way to her cottage. Virginia stared after her, trying to think of what came next, but in her exhaustion, the only next step she could come up with was to sleep.

THE NEXT MORNING began with a condo viewing with Jack and Stephanie. Stephanie brought with her a thermos of tea and looked longingly at Jack's travel mug of coffee the entire drive.

"We can stop and get you some coffee," Virginia suggested from the back seat.

Stephanie insisted she was fine, that she actually preferred tea, but she was on edge and cranky the entire morning. Virginia tried to leave her alone about it—she'd tried cutting out caffeine a few times over the years to ease stomach troubles or insomnia, and the last thing she'd wanted then was well-meaning people offering coffee or commenting on her abstinence—but it was hard. Every criticism Virginia had of the condo was met with disagreement or hostility from an uncaffeinated Stephanie, until Virginia stopped voicing her opinions entirely. It didn't help that in the back of her mind, Virginia was waiting to be arrested at any moment for her little stunt at Cindy's the night before.

"I just don't think this is the right solution for me," Virginia said, eager to wrap up the visit. "I don't want to live alone in a home that's not my house."

"Mom, your house is gone." Virginia flinched, and Jack made a face like his comment had come out harsher than he intended. More softly, he said, "We'll work with you to make sure wherever you choose to live feels like home. We want you to be happy, but we also want you to consider all the options."

"I've considered it, and I don't think a condo with in-home care is the right option for me." Truthfully, Breeze Village was the only option Virginia had really let herself consider wholeheartedly. She'd thought about Harbor Vale, and the social atmosphere of a place like that still sounded better than living alone in a house while making peace with needing assistance, but it was across town from Breeze Village and her friends. Instead of living minutes from Marney, she'd be living with Jan, watching her black beehive hair-do bob back and forth every morning while Jan cornered her to gossip together.

When Jack finally decided there was no value in staying any longer, Virginia took off toward Breeze

Village. She hadn't stopped wondering about Marney's declaration that Colleen wasn't liaising with the spirit world any longer.

The lobby was bustling. Family members were visiting their loved ones, residents were enjoying card games, and a sing-along session was at full volume in one of the activities rooms off the lobby. Virginia checked in quickly, making her way toward the elevator. The noise and crowds were overwhelming, and she focused on the questions she wanted to ask Colleen to center herself as she walked through the busy space.

"Watch where you're going!"

Too late. Virginia collided with another body and looked up to see Liam glowering at her.

"I'm so sorry!"

"You ought to be. What are you even doing here, anyway?"

"I came to visit my friends."

"I don't know why you're even allowed back here. Michelle should have stuck to her guns after you assaulted a resident. Now that we add 'murder suspect' to the list of your lovely qualities, you're free to come and go as you please?" He let out a huff of breath and took off, stalking across the room without waiting for a response from Virginia.

A lump formed in Virginia's throat, and she bit her tongue to keep tears from springing to her eyes. Suddenly it was hard to remember what she'd come for. She just wanted to turn around and leave.

"Virginia!" A cheerful voice drew her attention, and

Virginia turned to see Ronald making his way to the dining room. "Care for a game of cards?"

Virginia forced a smile, or the closed approximation she could manage, as she shook her head. She started to turn, but through the French doors behind Ronald, she could see Gemma and Colleen in the courtyard gardens.

"Not today," she said. "Next time, though."

"I'll hold you to that."

Ronald's toothless grin was a small relief. Friend. He was her friend, and he cared about her. He didn't resent her for accidentally assaulting him with hot tea, and he didn't think she was a murderer.

Virginia clung to those thoughts as she made her way toward Gemma and Colleen in the garden. "Colleen!" she called.

Gemma and Colleen turned and gave her a small wave but hurried off toward Gemma's cottage before she reached them. Virginia frowned and started after them. If Colleen wasn't using her abilities any longer, that was fine, but Virginia was going to make her say so herself.

She'd just reached Gemma's cottage, hand raised to knock on the door, when Haley came hurrying out of the dining room and into the courtyard.

"Virginia!" Haley's voice was frantic and her face was pale. Her false lashes exaggerated the way her eyes were wide with surprise or disbelief, and Virginia thought she looked equal parts comical and terrifying.

"What's wrong?"

But Virginia had hardly gotten the words out when she saw two uniformed officers following Haley out of the building, their eyes fixed on Virginia. They didn't look panicked. They looked calm, cool, and collected. They looked like they meant business.

This was it, she thought. They'd caught her for her stupid stunt breaking into Cindy's house.

"Virginia Walker?" one of them asked.

Virginia nodded. Swallowing suddenly became difficult, and she wasn't sure she could walk if she tried.

"We'd like to ask you a few questions about the murder of Michelle Martin."

Virginia stood still, any potential response frozen in her throat.

"Would you mind coming with us down to the station?"

Still too stunned to give a proper response, Virginia only nodded. Before she could process what was happening, the officers stepped to either side of her and were leading her back through the courtyard toward the main building and the parking lot. She turned and saw both Colleen and Gemma watching through a window in Gemma's cottage. In the dining room, conversations had quieted, and all eyes were on Virginia as the officers practically carried her through the space, supporting her on each arm. Her legs felt like jelly, and every time she took a step she nearly fell over.

Though she knew the room had gone silent, the world seemed loud in Virginia's ears. A high-pitched ringing took over, and everything else sounded muffled. Then, in the background, a phone rang. The sound made Virginia's heart speed up but she wasn't sure why. It sounded familiar. If she could only place a finger on it, only single out the sound in the chaos.

"Whose phone is that?" Virginia choked out.

Haley looked surprised. "It's Michelle's. She must have left it in her desk."

And in that moment, as the officers carted her out the door and helped her into the back of one of their cars, Virginia placed the ringtone. She'd definitely heard it before—in Russ's room while she was hiding in a closet.

CHAPTER 12

Virginia wouldn't remember the drive to the police station. She wouldn't remember following the officers into a tiny interrogation room, speaking her name and date of birth into a tape recorder, then waiting for the questioning to begin. It was all too much. Too much on top of the realization that Michelle had been the intruder she'd been hiding from. Michelle had been at the casino that day. Michelle was now dead, and for some reason, Virginia was supposed to have killed her.

"What's going on here?"

Virginia turned her head, half in a stupor, and saw a wild-eyed Dylan rushing into the room. One of the officers took Dylan aside and they conversed in low voices. Virginia was too out of it to care that they were talking about her as if she wasn't there. She was likely the least-informed person in the room about the crime she'd allegedly committed.

She was vaguely aware as Dylan pulled out her phone

and called her kids. Heard Jack's name, then Lucy's, on Dylan's lips. She was too dazed to feel panic, to worry about what her kids would say. Somewhere between seeing those cops and knowing she was going to be arrested for breaking and entering and the arrival at the police station to be questioned for murder, Virginia felt like she'd left her body. She watched the events play out but didn't feel connected to them. Didn't worry about the consequences, because those consequences applied to a body she no longer fully inhabited.

"Wait here."

Dylan's voice was gruff, and she half-snatched the two other officers by their collars and pulled them from the room, slamming the door shut behind them. She left Virginia alone for a few minutes before returning with a Styrofoam cup of coffee.

"Here."

She pushed the cup of coffee across the table to Virginia. Virginia looked at it, then at Dylan, then back at the cup before picking it up and bringing it to her lips. The aroma filled her nostrils, the smell grounding her slightly, pulling her back into her body.

The coffee was thick and tasted burnt. It burned her tongue on the first sip, and after that, Virginia couldn't taste it as she forced down the rest.

"We need to talk." Dylan leveled her gaze at Virginia.

Virginia set down the empty cup and returned Dylan's gaze. Then she blinked and looked around, taking in the space for the first time. The room was small, the walls painted a dull gray, a metal table and two chairs the only furniture occupying the space. Fluorescent lights in the drop ceiling flickered. The wall opposite Virginia was largely made up of a window she couldn't see through. She wondered if there were cops on the other side watching her. If they could hear her conversation with Dylan.

"No one's watching," Dylan said as if she could read Virginia's mind. "And I turned off the recorder."

"What's going on?" Virginia asked, looking away from the window and returning her gaze to Dylan.

Dylan stared back at her, her lips pulled down in a tight frown. "I was going to ask you the same thing."

"Michelle. She's dead?"

Dylan nodded.

"Why do they think I did it?"

Dylan's frown deepened. "I'm not supposed to tell you anything." She and Virginia looked at each other in silence, Dylan looking torn, before she finally continued. "Just don't get me in trouble."

Virginia nodded, eager to hear whatever Dylan had decided to divulge.

"Were you with Michelle yesterday?"

Virginia shook her head but narrowed her eyes at Dylan. "Are you interrogating me now?"

Dylan stood up and raised her hands to her head, letting out an exasperated sigh. "Virginia, your necklace was at the crime scene."

Virginia's breath caught in her throat.

"In Michelle's hand."

"What does that mean?"

"It looks like you were in a fight. It looks like you

attacked her, and she grabbed your necklace. It looks like you killed her."

Virginia was speechless, a rarity for her. She hadn't been with Michelle. Hadn't even known she was dead. Her hand unconsciously flew to her neck, and she was surprised to find it bare. The necklace her children had given her for Mother's Day was gone. Her eyes widened at the realization, and Dylan nodded.

"I'm not sure how many other people in Seaview have a necklace engraved with both yours and your kids' names."

Probably not many.

"You weren't with her?" Dylan asked again.

Virginia shook her head.

"You need an attorney. This doesn't look good for you."

* * *

Virginia dozed off after being left alone in the interrogation room. The next thing she knew, the door was flung open violently, snatching her from sleep, and both her children rushed in. Jack held his phone to his ear, his eyes wild. His hair was disheveled and his shirt was wrinkled. Virginia couldn't recall the last time she'd seen him look so not put-together. Lucy's heels clicked on the floor as she rushed over to Virginia and threw her arms around her.

"Mom, you're okay," she breathed into Virginia's neck as she hugged her. Her body was shaking.

"I'm okay," Virginia answered, hugging her daughter

back. She stroked her hand up and down Lucy's back and repeated the words. "I'm okay. It's okay. Everything is okay."

The urge to comfort her daughter was profound, and for a moment, she forgot why they were there.

"Thanks, I'll talk with you soon." Jack hung up the phone and turned his attention to his mother and sister in their embrace. "Mom, what the hell?"

Virginia released Lucy and looked up at her son. Fury shone in his eyes. She didn't know how to respond.

"How did this happen?" A pleading look spread across Jack's face. He wasn't just angry; he looked sad and confused and terrified. And seeing that look on his face made Virginia's stomach drop.

"I don't know," she said quietly. "Dylan said my necklace… Michelle had it somehow? I never touched her. I haven't seen her in days."

Jack cursed and began to pace. Virginia looked at Lucy, whose eyes were bloodshot and kept looking at the floor and the ceiling to avoid Virginia's eyes.

The door swung open, the metal handle smacking into the wall. Dylan came in and flashed Jack and Lucy an apologetic smile.

"I do have a small update. It might help." All eyes and ears were on Dylan as she continued. "We got an estimated time of death for Michelle from the Medical Examiner. Half past six last night."

All eyes and ears were on Virginia then as she considered where she was at the time, whether she had an alibi.

"The good news is, I was definitely not with Michelle

then," she said, cringing. "The bad news is that I may have been somewhere I wasn't supposed to be."

Dylan put her hands over her ears and turned toward the door. "I'm not hearing this!" She pulled the door closed behind her, and Jack turned his face back to Virginia.

In a lowered voice, Jack said, "Not in a goddamned interrogation room. There are microphones."

When her kids had kindly informed the officers that Virginia would not be answering any further questions and shuffled her out of the station and into the dying light of the evening, Jack wheeled on her.

"Talk," he spat.

Virginia flinched and wiped his spittle from her face. "I broke into someone's house."

"You what?" Lucy was aghast.

Virginia recounted select details from her investigation so far: that Russ's wife had acted strange in the aftermath of his death and that she'd found evidence of Michelle and Cindy being connected in some way. That she'd broken into Cindy's home and discovered that Michelle was trying to buy back Breeze Village at a profit after Russ died and she'd publicly announced illegal activity taking place there, tarnishing the reputation of the place.

When she'd finished, Jack stood silently, mouth hanging slightly open.

Lucy threw her arms up in the air, apoplectic. "Great! You have an alibi! You couldn't have been murdering the dead woman because instead, you were breaking and entering, something illegal that you also did alone and no one can vouch for! Phenomenal!"

"I told Marney and Lawrence right after." Virginia's voice was quiet.

Neither of her kids responded.

"Michelle was also at the casino the weekend Russ was killed." Virginia left out the details of how she knew that —the snooping in Russ's room. "She was up to something. I know it."

"Whatever Michelle might have been involved in, she's dead, and it looks like you killed her. And not just her, but the other sketchy dead guy, too." Jack's voice was practically a growl.

Virginia felt weak at the knees, the gravity of the situation tugging at her. She wobbled, then reached out to stabilize herself on a parked car. Its alarm immediately sounded, causing the three of them to startle. Jack cursed again, and Lucy took Virginia's arm in her own.

"Come on, Mom," she said softly, the way she might comfort a child who'd had a meltdown. "Let's get you home. We can talk more later."

Virginia wanted to go to Marney's place instead of spending another night in Jack's guest room, but she didn't dare ask. Marney had enough on her plate, healing her own trauma and working toward opening her crochet shop—something that was hers and hers alone. And Virginia had done enough, summoning her to Lawrence's the night before and making her fear the worst. She needed to let her be.

But as she stared out the window in the back seat of Jack's car, she couldn't help but long for her best friend.

Though Marney didn't always agree with Virginia, she'd never once made Virginia feel misunderstood or unheard. And that night, Virginia wanted to curl up beside her friend in bed and feel Marney stroke her hair like she'd done after Earl passed. She wanted Marney to tell her that she was strong enough to navigate this part of her life.

Had her car not been at Breeze Village, left behind when she was stuffed into a cop car and driven away in full view of everyone, Virginia would have made the drive to Marney's. She would have knocked on her door and poured out everything that was weighing her down, even if she knew it wasn't the right thing to do. Instead, she was stranded.

As she lay in bed, she could hear Jack pacing in the living room, his low voice as he talked on the phone to someone Virginia guessed was an attorney Jack was trying to hire for her. Stephanie had already been in bed when they'd arrived home.

She thought about what Stephanie pictured when she married Jack, whether she'd ever imagined that his mother would be living with them, would insert herself into murder investigations and get herself carted off to the police station. She wondered if Stephanie resented her presence. If she felt the way Virginia knew Jack felt, but just hid it better behind her kind and bubbly façade. The thought made her feel nauseated.

While sleep eluded her, Virginia reached over to the nightstand and pulled open the tiny drawer. She extracted the small, plastic hotel key she'd kept for herself when handing over the phones to the officer. It was the one thing she'd kept for herself, and she clung tight to it, running her fingers over the smooth surface until finally exhaustion won out and she fell asleep.

* * *

VIRGINIA SLEPT FITFULLY MOST of the night, and then solidly most of the morning. When a soft knock at her door woke her, it was nearly noon. The sun peeked around the edges of the curtains. A second knock came as she oriented herself, reminding herself of where she was, of what had happened to her. Irritation rose in her alongside dread for the conversation she knew she and Jack were about to have. But the knock was too soft, too kind, she realized, to have been Jack. And he would have barged in after the first went unanswered.

"Come in."

The door opened, and Marney poked her head in, her neat gray curls framing a worried face. She was made up with vibrant lipstick and sparkling earrings, and they stood in contrast to her nervous expression. Her skin was so pale it looked almost green, and dark circles were visible through the concealer under her eyes.

"Virginia." Marney practically breathed her name, stepping fully into the room and wrapping Virginia in an embrace before Virginia could say anything.

As soon as she felt the comfort of her friend's arms around her, Virginia dissolved into tears. Marney pulled back the curtains, letting the midday sun stream into the room, and Lawrence knocked at the doorframe before joining them.

"We brought biscuits." Lawrence gestured over his

shoulder toward the kitchen, and Virginia sniffed the air for the aromas of breakfast someone else—someone more skilled in the kitchen—prepared so she didn't have to.

"And this was on the door."

Lawrence handed Virginia a small sticky note. In Jack's handwriting, it read *Heading out for an appointment. Please don't go anywhere. -J*

Virginia scoffed at being told what to do. She crumpled the note and tossed it in the trash.

With her face washed and teeth brushed, Virginia felt herself coming alive again. When she walked into the kitchen, the full impact of the breakfast scents—coffee and sausage and biscuits and cinnamon rolls—brought her the rest of the way to life.

"Do you want to talk about it?" Lawrence waited to ask the question until Virginia had drunk half her mug of coffee.

"What have you guys heard?" Virginia wanted to know.

Marney looked to Lawrence before answering. "Gemma came straight to my cottage after... you know. She just said she thought you'd been arrested, but she didn't know for what, and she wasn't sure if you were really arrested since they didn't handcuff you. She said Haley had been there so I asked her, and she told me what she knew."

"They didn't arrest me. At least, I don't think so. Just brought me in for questioning. How much does the rest of Breeze Village know?"

"Everything, I think." Marney cringed as she delivered the news, but Virginia hadn't expected anything less.

Heck, if she'd witnessed something that exciting, she wouldn't be keeping it to herself. The gossip was half the appeal of living in a community like Breeze Village.

The three sat in silence, Marney and Lawrence following Virginia's lead. Finally, Virginia said, "I just don't get it."

She chewed her food and the others waited for her to go on.

"How can Bo's Biscuits taste so *good?* It's just biscuits! I make biscuits, but they don't taste like these."

Marney's face relaxed and her shoulders dropped.

"But also Michelle," Virginia continued. "She had my necklace."

"You think someone planted it?" Lawrence asked.

Virginia shrugged. "At the casino, I assumed I'd just lost my nail file and someone opportunistic found it and decided to stab Russ to death with it. I mean, it's bizarre, but it seemed more likely than someone intentionally framing me for murder. But now... I don't think this time was accidental."

"Who would want to frame you?" Marney asked, brows furrowed.

Virginia shook her head. "I did accuse Ronald and Haley of murder this spring, but they both seem to have pretty well gotten over it. And Jack and Stephanie are certainly ready to have me out of here, but I don't think they're trying to boot me from here into a penitentiary somewhere."

Marney frowned. "I'm being serious. I can't make it make sense."

Virginia was surprised. Marney had always been

adamantly against Virginia investigating. Virginia expected Marney's response to be *Cooperate with the police, and it'll all work itself out.*

"You turned over Russ's phones to that detective. Maybe they had vital information, and now the police are onto Russ's killer. Maybe the killer wanted to make sure everyone is looking into you, not him."

"Or her," Lawrence added. When Virginia and Marney turned to him, he put his hands up. "Women are just as capable of taking out their enemies as men."

"But would a woman have stabbed him to death?" Marney cocked her head to the side as if she were thinking about it. "I think a woman would have just poisoned him. Less messy."

"I thought you thought it was the wife?"

Virginia sat back and listened to her friends' back-and-forth with astonishment. "Aren't you guys supposed to be telling me to sit back, stop speculating, and let the police do their thing?"

Marney jutted her chin out. "That was before the police's 'thing' was hauling you off to jail for something you didn't do."

CHAPTER 13

At a stoplight that afternoon, after Lawrence had taken her to Breeze Village to pick up her car, Virginia pulled out her phone and dialed a number she'd never thought she'd call again. It rang six times before Detective Foster picked up.

"Foster speaking."

Virginia's stomach turned at the sound of his voice, and before she could stop herself, she hung up the phone. She thought she might be sick, and she concentrated on her breathing as the light turned green and she resumed driving.

It wasn't until she'd reached her destination that she could bring herself to call the detective again, and it was only as a procrastination tactic to avoid going inside.

"Who is this?" Foster's voice was harsh on the other end of the line.

"Detective Foster, this is Virginia Walker." Virginia's voice wavered. She straightened her back as much as she could in the car seat, pulling her shoulders back and raising her chin in hopes that the pose would imbue her voice with confidence.

"What do you want?"

"I wanted to check in on the phones I gave you. I wanted to see whether there had been any leads that came from them."

"I'm not authorized to disclose that information. Now, if there's nothing else—"

Virginia cut him off before he could end the conversation and hang up the phone. "Wait! Did you hear about Michelle Martin's murder?"

"I did."

A pause stretched over the line.

Virginia took in another deep breath and raised her chin a degree higher. "I believe the person who killed Russ is likely the person who killed Michelle. At the very least, I believe the murders are connected. And I'm being framed for Michelle's murder, whether that was Russ's killer's original intention or not."

No response from Detective Foster.

Virginia continued. "Russ's wife, Cindy, was connected to both victims. If you have any leads on her or anyone else, it would—"

"Let me stop you right there," Foster said. "There is one murder case in my jurisdiction, not two. And you are a suspect in that case. So far, you're a suspect who can't stay away. That doesn't make you look better, and asking me to divulge privileged information is certainly not a good look. Goodbye now."

The detective hung up and Virginia sat in the car, still holding her phone to her ear after the line had gone dead.

She looked up and out the windshield at the building before her. The plain brick building had once been a bank. A two-lane drive-thru still stuck off one side of the building. The bank sign had been replaced with big green lettering: *Murphy, Benoit, & Davidson.*

Let's get this over with. Virginia lifted herself from the car. Her groans were only half induced by the effort of angling herself out of the car, the other half by the conversation ahead of her.

JACK HAD SET up a meeting with the Murphy of Murphy, Benoit, & Davidson. He was a small man with a surprisingly strong handshake, decked out in an impeccably tailored suit, an ostentatiously bedazzled watch, and rings on nearly every finger with gemstones of various size, color, and cut. Virginia's gaze wandered, and when it returned to the attorney's face, he wore a satisfied smile. He liked being appraised.

"Mrs. Walker. My time is expensive. Let's get right to it."

Mr. Murphy gestured to a chair across a large mahogany desk from his own gorgeous leather chair. Virginia looked at it—worn yellow upholstery with little red pineapples dotting the fabric—and sat. Like most of the furniture and decor adorning the office, it seemed expensive but dated. Luxury from the '90s.

Her attorney waited until she'd sat down, then nodded at her and rested his chin on his folded hands, elbows on the desk in front of him. "Right. Let's start with what happened."

"The police think I killed a woman. Michelle Martin." Virginia recounted, to the best of her ability, being brought in for questioning.

The attorney frowned, taking notes throughout her story. "And they believe you murdered this woman why? Did you threaten her? Were you seen with her shortly before her death?"

"She had my necklace. That's what Dylan said. She's my friend's daughter, basically family, and she's the Assistant Chief of Police here in Seaview. She said Michelle had my necklace in her hand, that it looked like she'd ripped it from her attacker. So they presume that attacker was me."

"And what is your side of the story?"

"I didn't kill her, obviously."

"Do you have an alibi?"

Virginia hesitated.

"Attorney-client privilege. You can tell me anything. No need to worry."

She squirmed. "I wasn't with anyone. I was... I was breaking into someone else's house to snoop around."

The attorney looked up from his notepad for the first time since their conversation began. "Tell me more."

So she did. Virginia recounted the story of breaking into Cindy's house, including backing up and telling Mr. Murphy how she was also a suspect in Russ's murder investigation to explain why she felt the need to smash through Cindy's window and poke around her house.

By the end of the story, her attorney wasn't even

trying to take notes. He was staring at her, mouth hanging slightly agape, eyes growing wider with every sentence she spoke. The two looked at each other for a moment and then he popped his mouth shut and gave her a smile that looked rehearsed.

"Well, alrighty, then. It's not the wildest story I've heard."

"Erm, what do you think my chances are? I'm not going to jail for this, am I?"

Mr. Murphy maintained his dazzling smile as he shook his head. "Nothing to worry about. I'm very good at my job, Mrs. Walker. I've gotten guiltier people out of trouble plenty of times."

Virginia's stomach churned. "But I'm not guilty. I didn't kill Michelle."

"See, we've got our stories straight already."

Virginia excused herself. Bile rose in her throat, and she held onto the wall outside the office to steady herself.

"Can I help you, ma'am?" A young, smartly-dressed secretary approached Virginia.

Virginia shook her head and hurried back out to her car, driving away without looking back.

* * *

"How could you?" Virginia was hardly inside the house when she blew up at her son. "What did you do, search for the most vile attorney you could find?"

"What are you talking about?" Jack looked genuinely surprised, but it did nothing to quell Virginia's anger.

"That was humiliating! My own attorney all but told

me he didn't believe my story, that he thinks I'm guilty but is more than happy to lie his ass off to keep me out of jail."

Jack paced, rubbing his face with his hands as he let out an exasperated exhale. "It's fine," he said after a moment. "I'll get you a new attorney."

"I don't want a new attorney! I want the cops to listen to me and not charge me in the first place."

"I understand. But we have to be prepared."

Virginia opened her mouth to respond, one hand on her hip and the other pointing a finger at Jack, ready to tear into him, when Stephanie rounded the corner and started shouting.

"You two have been at each other's throats, and I have had it! That's enough! You're stressing me out, and I can't take it anymore. Virginia, you're getting a goddamned attorney, and that's that. When you get yourself accused of murder, you get the joy of dealing with legal representation. Jack, find her another flipping lawyer. And both of you stop being assholes to each other."

She disappeared back down the hallway, her ponytail whipping as she turned on her heel. Both Jack and Virginia stood stock still, stunned into silence.

Finally Jack mumbled, "I'll find another attorney and let you know." He stalked off after his wife and Virginia retreated to her car. The way she saw it, she could either spend the rest of her day alone, stewing in her anger, or she could stew in her anger at Breeze Village and maybe win some money off Ronald in a poker game to take the edge off the day. The second option sounded better than the first.

* * *

WHEN RONALD DEFEATED her four rounds in a row, Virginia's idea to pass the rest of the day playing poker at Breeze Village didn't seem so great anymore.

"You've got to be kidding me!" By this point, her cheerful façade was slipping and her irritation shone through.

"You okay?" Ronald peered warily over at Virginia as he shuffled the cards, and she shrugged.

"It's been a day."

"I bet. I know about… I mean, I heard…"

"It's okay. The cops brought me in for questioning. People saw me leave with the police and think I was arrested. It's fine. My reputation was already iffy."

Ronald looked relieved. "I was just real sorry to hear. I mean, I know you didn't do it. And with Russ an' all, it's just a lot on your shoulders right now."

Virginia looked around the room. A few other tables were occupied, but the occupees seemed sufficiently engrossed in their own card games and conversations.

"I learned something about Michelle. Right before she died. She was trying to buy back Breeze Village."

Ronald paused shuffling and looked at her in confusion. "What do you mean?"

"She made an offer to Cindy to buy the place back. And she wasn't the only one."

Ronald leaned in closer, enraptured, and Virginia enjoyed the little buzz of sharing information, of knowing something no one else knew and then telling someone.

"Hashim, the owner of Harbor Vale, made an offer, too."

At this, Ronald leaned back in his chair, pressing against the table with both hands. He exhaled loudly. "Are you sure?"

Virginia nodded. "I thought Michelle was so crazy going on TV talking about those kickbacks or whatever, but now I'm wondering if she wasn't trying to hurt the reputation of this place to buy it back for less than she sold it for."

Ronald leaned his head from side to side like he was weighing multiple options. "It's possible. And Cindy'd probably be more willing to sell a place if it was caught up in an investigation. Someone was just telling me there was 'bout to be an investigation starting into all that mess. The FBI or something."

Virginia's eyes widened. She needed to verify that little tidbit before she spread the rumor further, but wouldn't that be something?

"How'd you find this out, anyway?" Ronald wanted to know.

"I can't say. Only that I know it with complete certainty."

Ronald considered this as he went back to shuffling the cards, then dealt out another round.

"Anyway, I can't figure out how it all fits together. Cindy seemed so unfazed by Russ's death, I thought for sure she did it. But then Marney made a good point about how women prefer poisoning to stabbing, and also I can't think of why Cindy would kill Michelle."

"Why does the same person have to have killed 'em both?"

"Well, I've been framed for two murders, so I'm assuming it's the same person that did them both."

"You know, I heard from Dick that Hashim tried to buy Breeze Village from Michelle before. When she sold it to Russ. He's trying to expand and create a second location for Harbor Vale or something. The deal was basically done and then Russ swooped in with a better offer and bought it out from under him."

Virginia looked up at him in disbelief. "How does Dick know that?"

"He's friends with Hashim, I think. Got a lot of pre-retirement friends that live over in Harbor Vale so he spends a lot of time over there."

"With Russ gone, it seems Cindy didn't have any desire to keep this place. So Hashim gets another chance to buy it, but then Michelle comes in trying to buy it back. And now she's dead, too."

Virginia was too excited to remember to keep her cards concealed. She could hardly sit still. Ronald looked equal parts excited and nervous. He took advantage of Virginia's distraction and won another round, then set his cards down at looked at her.

"You gonna go over to Harbor Vale and investigate?"

"How could I not?" Virginia's legs bounced under the table. She felt ready to run there herself.

"Just be careful."

CHAPTER 14

"I think I'd like to go visit Harbor Vale."

Both Jack and Stephanie stopped mid-bite and stared at Virginia like she'd just sprouted horns.

"What?"

"The situation with Breeze Village isn't going to resolve itself. You guys are right that I need to start considering other options, and Harbor Vale might be better than I've been assuming."

Jack narrowed his eyes. "You said you—"

Stephanie kicked him under the table, jostling the dishes, and cut him off. "That's wonderful! We'd love to visit with you."

Virginia beamed. "How about tomorrow?"

The reality was that the only person Virginia knew at Harbor Vale was Jan, and a tour as a prospective resident seemed like a more enjoyable way to get in and poke around than visiting her. And it had the side benefit of making Jack and Stephanie feel good, thinking she was opening up her heart to options beyond Breeze Village.

On the drive over there, Jack cleared his throat. "You know, Mom, this is really good timing. We were going to bring it up last night at dinner. Stephanie and I have been talking, and Lucy, too, and we wanted to pick a date that we thought would be doable for you to find a place you like. We think having a date in mind would be a good thing."

A knot formed in Virginia's stomach. An eviction date. That's what he was saying.

"It's not a big deal," he said, sensing her displeasure. "We just think it would be good for all of us to have a timeline."

"Of course."

The rest of the drive was quiet, and when they pulled up to Harbor Vale and parked, Virginia was eager to get out of the cramped, tense car. She had hardly taken three steps into the lobby when a familiar voice cried, "Is that who I think it is?"

She looked up to see Jan bobbing toward her, hair balanced precariously atop her head, jewelry jingling with every step. Beside her was Dorothea, her hair far more subdued but her wrists stacked with even more jangly bracelets than Jan's. The pair of them could have single-handedly put on a Christmas show with their musical trimmings.

"Hello!" Virginia tried to sound excited. She didn't remember Dorothea moving here, but at this point, it was hard to keep track.

Dorothea wrapped Virginia in a hug. "What are you doing here?"

"I came to check out the place. See my options, appease my kids, you know."

She tried to force a cheeky smile. The memory of their neighborhood tea party in which she'd discovered the whole neighborhood had agreed to sell their homes came back to her. She'd felt so embarrassed, and now being seen here felt like being wrong all over again. There was Virginia, trying to fight a property development company with practically unlimited resources, and now here she was three months later finally facing the music.

"Well, we would be blessed if you moved in here, isn't that so?" Jan said.

Dorothea nodded. "I come visit Jan whenever I get lonely in my condo. I don't know how much longer I'll stay. I'm here so often I figure I should just take the plunge and make it permanent."

"I have to say, I've never once regretted it. And none of that chaos that Breeze Village has been going through." Jan gave Virginia a pointed look, and Virginia flushed.

"It is crazy over there," she agreed. "But I actually need to get back to my son and his wife. We're going to talk with the owner and have a little tour. It was lovely seeing you."

Virginia turned to where Jack and Stephanie were standing. They were smiling at her as if they were parents dropping their toddler off at preschool, thrilled to see her making friends and fitting in.

"You don't need to come with us," Jack said. "We can talk with him, and you can spend some time with your friends."

Jan and Dorothea lit up like it was a lovely idea.

"There's a flower arranging class starting in just a minute. We were on our way there when we saw you," Jan said.

"That sounds perfect. Why don't you go do that and we'll come find you for the tour after we talk with the owner?"

Virginia couldn't protest without looking childish, so she reluctantly went with Jan and Dorothea.

"I'm so glad you get to do this with us," Jan said, giving Virginia a conspiratorial look. "I wanted to get the latest on everything at Breeze Village from you."

Of course, she did.

"I don't really want to talk about it."

Dorothea gave her a sympathetic look. "We heard about your... the arrest." She whispered the word *arrest*, looking around to make sure no one would overhear.

"Just a misunderstanding." Virginia forced an unconcerned shrug. "I wasn't arrested. They just wanted me to come in for questioning. It turned out to be nothing, really."

Jan and Dorothea nodded solemnly.

A young man cleared his throat and announced the class was starting. The room they were in was carpeted, with tables set up all throughout, each full of floral supplies. Jan had led their group to a table on the side of the room.

Once class was underway, Virginia leaned in and whispered, "So what do you two know about the owner here?"

"Not much," Jan said.

"But I'd like to get to know him, if you know what I mean." Dorothea waggled her eyebrows, thin semi-circles drawn in harsh dark pencil above her eyes.

"I'd hold off on that," Virginia said without thinking.

Both Jan and Dorothea gave her a questioning look.

"I just have my suspicions. I was hoping to chat with him while I was here. You know, a little investigative work."

"You think he killed Russ?" Jan's whisper was hardly that, and the next table over turned to look at them.

Virginia gave them a small wave and they turned back to their flower arrangements. Jan whispered an apology.

"What about Michelle?" Dorothea asked. "You think he did her, too?"

"I don't know."

"Was he even there when Russ was killed?"

"I don't know," Virginia repeated. "Hence the need for more investigation. But, just… hold off on ditching your hot younger man for him for a little while, at least."

When the class ended, Virginia bid Jan and Dorothea goodbye and went to find Jack and Stephanie and hopefully Hashim. She returned to the lobby, a carpeted octagonal space much less reminiscent of a hospital than Breeze Village's lobby but also much less bustling with life and conversation.

She found Jack and Stephanie standing in the center of the room next to a small table that held decorative vases. Next to them was a man she assumed to be Hashim. He confirmed it a moment later when he held out his hand and introduced himself.

"It's nice to meet you. I was just telling your son and

his wife that I won't be able to take you all on the tour today, but Mandy would be delighted to. She's worked here for years and knows the place inside and out."

Virginia didn't let her face betray her disappointment, instead smiling and thanking him. She turned to Jack, but before she could say anything, the door opened in her periphery and she turned to see Dick strolling through the door with his walker.

"Dick, my man!" Hashim crossed the room and clapped Dick on the back.

This time, Virginia stood no chance at concealing the emotions on her face. Her mouth opened slightly as she saw Dick and Hashim exchange friendly greetings. Ronald had said they were friends, but she hadn't expected them to be this close.

Dick offered Virginia half a wave as he made his way to the front desk to check in and then over to the elevators.

"Are you ready?" Stephanie's cheery voice startled Virginia.

"Just one second. I forgot something."

She hurriedly returned to the room where the flower arranging class had taken place and breathed a sigh of relief when she saw Jan and Dorothea still there, talking with a handful of other seniors. They looked at her in surprise as she approached, huffing and puffing.

"I just saw Dick in the lobby. From Breeze Village."

Jan looked unsurprised. "He's got a handful of friends here. Comes over a lot."

Virginia nodded. "Have you seen him with the owner

before? The way he greeted Dick, they just seemed really close."

"Well, I don't really know about that. I guess they're friends." Jan shrugged.

"You know what I heard?" Dorothea chimed in.

Both Jan and Virginia looked at her impatiently.

"Dick's son is a doctor. He just had to close down his practice after Michelle's announcement on TV. Apparently, he was one of the ones involved." Dorothea glowed with the joy of spreading gossip. Virginia was sure her and Jan's shocked faces only amplified Dorothea's gratification.

Jan started to pepper Dorothea with questions, but Virginia felt her head spinning and excused herself.

"Ready?" Jack was waiting in the lobby, restless, both hands on his hips. A woman in scrubs whose name tag said *Mandy* was chatting with Stephanie.

"I'm actually not feeling really well," Virginia said. "I think I need to go home."

Jack's frown deepened. He didn't do well with last-minute changes to the plan. But to Virginia's surprise, he took three deep breaths and then put on his best approximation of a smile.

"Well, then, I suppose we've got to get going. Our apologies for the inconvenience."

He shook Mandy's hand and then led the way back to the car, Virginia staring after him in confusion. *Since when does Jack take deep breaths instead of exploding when things don't go his way?*

* * *

AT DINNER THAT NIGHT, Jack was quiet, but his jaw kept clenching.

"What's the matter?" Virginia wanted to know.

"Nothing, it's not important."

"Oh, come on. Something's clearly bothering you."

Jack set his fork down and stared across the table at Virginia. Stephanie lowered her eyes, suddenly extremely interested in her potatoes.

"What's the matter? That asshole who owns Harbor Vale doesn't want you in his place because of your reputation."

Virginia was stunned. "You all seemed totally fine after talking with him."

"I wasn't going to pitch a fit then and there," Jack said as if it were the most obvious thing in the world. Why display emotions in the moment when you can hold them in and clench your jaw about them hours later?

"You were going to take me on a tour and everything, knowing they wouldn't let me move in?"

"If we'd told you then, you'd have caused a scene. And besides, we didn't end up taking the tour."

"Well, that's all fine by me, anyway. The place has no character. It's not the right fit."

Stephanie kept her gaze averted. Jack stabbed a piece of chicken like it had personally insulted him.

"What is the right fit, Mom? A jail cell? Because that's where you seem to be trying to end up."

At that, Stephanie looked up, her face flushing. "Come on, Jack."

"No, it's all right," Virginia said. She set her fork down

and left the table, leaving her plate three-quarters full. Her appetite was gone, anyway.

* * *

Virginia rose before her kids and left the house quietly, creeping on her tiptoes until she was outside and had closed the door behind her. She climbed into her car and sped away. Her stomach grumbled, protesting going without much supper and without any breakfast, but she was on a mission.

She pulled into the police station alongside three other cars, each of them containing a sleepy officer reporting for duty. It being the height of summer, the sun was already well above the horizon, and the air felt heavy and thick. Clouds threatened another summer storm that afternoon. Virginia hurried inside so she could finish up here and be off the roads before then.

"I'm here to see Dylan Richards."

The man behind the desk, separated from Virginia by a piece of plexiglass, leaned in and asked her to repeat herself. With the divider between them, Virginia couldn't hear his request and asked him to repeat himself. After a few iterations, the man dialed Dylan's number on his phone and waved Virginia in the direction of her office. He seemed excited to be rid of her and back to his crossword.

Dylan frowned at Virginia as she entered the small office. The last time Virginia had been there, she'd been insistent that Dylan and her officers should be investigating Matt Beaumont for the murder of his mother. Dylan hadn't been thrilled to see her then, and she didn't seem thrilled to see her now, either. Virginia made a mental note to come by with cookies or something other than a request for information in the future, then filed that mental note away with the rest of them—in the mental equivalent of the junk drawer where things went in, never to be seen again.

"It's early," was all Dylan said by way of greeting.

"I was hoping you could help me."

"You know I can't. Not if it's about an active investigation. Especially not if it's about an active investigation in which you're a suspect."

Virginia sat without being invited to. "I know that. But it's important. You know I didn't kill Michelle. I don't even know where or how I supposedly did it! Everyone in Seaview has heard about me being brought in for questioning, and with this, plus Russ's murder at the bingo tournament, it's all too much. I went to visit Harbor Vale yesterday, and Jack said the owner won't let me move in because of my 'reputation.'"

Dylan narrowed her eyes. "You went to visit Harbor Vale?"

Virginia nodded.

"You're really looking at options beyond Breeze Village?"

Virginia nodded again. She figured it was okay to omit her true motive behind the visit to Harbor Vale since she was truly getting desperate enough to consider moving into Harbor Vale. She had a deadline now to get out of her kids' hair.

Dylan sighed. "I know that's hard for you." She nodded toward the door, signaling for Virginia to pull it shut, and Virginia did.

"This is a one-time thing," Dylan said.

Virginia nodded. Keeping quiet was working, and she wasn't about to say anything to risk making Dylan regret her decision.

"Michelle died by blunt force trauma to the head. No murder weapon found at the scene. As I told you before, your necklace was clutched in her hand. No other evidence like DNA or fibers has been found."

"So I'm supposed to have hit her over the head with something heavy? Well, doesn't that sort of rule me out? I'm not exactly in the best shape of my life."

Dylan leaned her head from side to side. "It does call into question your ability to commit the crime."

"And she's supposed to have reached out and grabbed at me while I'm coming at her with a weapon in my hands? I'd think she'd run away."

"No one knows how they'd respond in a situation like that until they're in one."

Virginia considered this. "And where was she killed?"

"At home."

"But doesn't she live at Breeze Village?"

Dylan exhaled, seemingly reconsidering sharing so much information. "She was living at Breeze Village, yes, but she has a house not too far from your old neighborhood with her husband."

"Husband?"

Dylan nodded.

"Why was she living at Breeze Village if she's got a

husband and a house? Why haven't I heard about the husband in all of this?"

Dylan stood. "I don't know the answers to either of those questions. I'm going to have to call an end to our little information session."

Virginia knew better than to protest. She stood and turned toward the door.

"We never had this conversation. And do *not* try to investigate. The best thing you can do is get yourself an attorney and keep out of trouble."

Virginia's face soured at the thought of her attorney.

Back in her car, Virginia felt hopeful. She had information. Whoever had killed Michelle had been strong enough to lift and hit her with something heavy. And Michelle had a husband. One she wasn't living with and hadn't been since Virginia met Michelle in the spring.

* * *

"Detective Foster, I think I may have some information for you." Virginia hadn't even left the police station parking lot before calling him.

"Oh, boy."

"I have information on the murder of Michelle from a reliable source. She was killed by blunt force trauma to the head. Is that something you already knew, and is it something you're following up on?"

The detective let out a long sigh, like it was taking everything he had not to start yelling. "I've told you before, that case isn't in our jurisdiction."

"But it narrows down the potential murderers to

people strong and able-bodied, and if it was the same killer for Russ and Michelle, that helps with your investigation into Russ's murder."

"The only reason we have to suspect that the same person killed Russ and Michelle is that identifying objects of yours were at both crime scenes."

Virginia flinched. "I couldn't have killed Michelle. I can hardly lift my arms above my head, and if I try to lift them both up at once, I go all wobbly. I'd have fallen over long before I could have bashed her head in."

"Mrs. Walker, I appreciate that you're trying to help. Well, I don't, but you understand. Please just let me and my officers do our jobs."

"Please." Virginia's voice was desperate. "I need to clear my name. It's making it impossible to find somewhere to live, and everyone is looking at me like I'm a horrible person, and I can't take it much longer."

Detective Foster didn't respond, but he didn't hang up, either.

"There's a man named Hashim Odeh who owns another senior living facility in Seaview. He had reason to want both Russ and Michelle gone. Maybe you could—"

The detective cut her off. "I understand you feel strongly about this case. But I need to remind you that the primary piece of evidence at the scene was your own nail file covered in the victim's blood. We're not going to just start bringing in anyone who's ever had a fight with the victim."

Virginia tried to protest, but Detective Foster cut her off again and then hung up on her.

Alone and fuming, she could only think of one thing to

do next: ignore Dylan's explicit instructions and see what the husband had to say for himself.

CHAPTER 15

Virginia drove toward her old neighborhood for five minutes before she realized she didn't actually know Michelle's address. She was contemplating going door to door, playing up the confused senior citizen angle until someone pointed her toward the correct house, when her phone chimed. A reminder flashed across the screen. *Condo viewing with Marney.* The investigation would have to wait, she supposed.

Visiting condos with Marney had been Lucy's idea. Apparently, Jack had told her how things had gone when Jack and Stephanie accompanied her to the previous viewing, and Lucy thought Marney might be better company. Virginia swung by Breeze Village to pick up Marney—she'd just gotten her new glasses but still needed to retake her tests to be road legal—and drove them to an area on the outskirts of downtown where a tiny little house had a "For Sale" sign in the yard.

"Isn't this cute!" Marney cooed over everything from

the roof to the footpath through the yard and only got more enthusiastic when they went inside.

"Look at this carpet!"

Virginia was less enthralled by the wall-to-wall royal blue carpet than Marney seemed to be.

"And this kitchen!"

The kitchen really was cute, although her lingering anger at the detective made her reluctant to admit it. It was dated—beige linoleum floors and oak cabinets—but the previous owner had painted the fronts of the cabinets different colors. Most were different shades of blue, with pops of tangerine. It was quirky in a way Virginia would never have dreamed up without seeing it first, but she loved it on sight.

"It's a little far from Breeze Village," she said, focusing on the too-bright carpet instead of the adorable kitchen.

"But so close to downtown! Oh, look how big this pantry is." Marney opened the pantry door. "I'm jealous!"

"You're the one who chose to move into your tiny cottage with no storage space."

Marney's eyes widened at Virginia's biting tone. She cleared her throat before leaving the kitchen and walking through the small living room.

"Nice little patio. Good space for a garden."

Marney's voice had lost its singsong excitement, but she was determined to point out all the good in this place. And there was a lot of good. The patio was small but covered, and the yard was small but well-maintained by the condo association. She could build and keep up with her garden but wouldn't have to worry about the regular yard work. The home was dated, sure, but it was no worse than her home had been before Jack had helped her sell it to Bellemeade. And with ample windows, the natural light was incredible.

Virginia just nodded.

"What is with you today?" Marney demanded.

"I had a crummy phone call with that detective, and I just can't shake the bad mood."

"Well, stop taking it out on me! Coming here wasn't my idea, and I've done nothing but try to see the positive."

"It wasn't my idea, either."

Marney and Virginia looked at each other, waiting to see who would back down first. Marney did.

"You called the detective again?"

Virginia opened her mouth to tell Marney about what Ronald had told her about Hashim trying to buy Breeze Village from Michelle the first time. About Dick and Hashim being friends. About Dick's son losing his medical practice thanks to Michelle. About how the killer had to have been strong and able-bodied enough to lift and swing a heavy object.

But before she could say any of that, Marney's phone rang. With an apologetic look, she stepped into the small bedroom to take the call. When she emerged, she apologized again.

"I have to go. I forgot I left my computer at the Best Buy and Jane was supposed to take me to pick it up. The Geek Gang or whatever they're called were going to work their magic since apparently I can't do a darn thing without getting a virus."

Happy enough to end the viewing early, Virginia drove Marney back to Breeze Village and watched her give Jane a warm embrace before climbing into her SUV and heading out. Jane, as if to make up for her own waif-like stature, drove a huge white Escalade that hardly fit inside a single lane.

Still in a sour mood, Virginia considered her next step before finally stepping out of the car and heading inside.

She stepped into the activities room where Patricia seemed to be leading a circle of women in a discussion of what, from the cover, looked to be a steamy romance. "Patricia." Virginia gestured for her to come over.

When Patricia stepped aside, Virginia asked her, "You didn't ever happen to see and photographically memorize Michelle's address, did you?"

"Sure," she said, as if it was the most obvious thing in the world. She spouted off the address and Virginia made her repeat it while she wrote it down. When she'd finished, Patricia asked, "May I ask why?"

"Did you know she has a husband?"

Patricia shook her head.

"Well, I didn't either until today, but I thought it would be nice and polite to go give him my condolences. Maybe bring him a casserole or something."

Patricia gave her a look that said *I see through your bull-shit* but went back to her book club. And just like that, Virginia had a lead.

WHATEVER VIRGINIA WAS EXPECTING when she knocked on Michelle's door, it wasn't the man who answered. Tall and easily 250 pounds, Michelle's husband could have been a lumberjack. Or a Viking. A Viking lumberjack who flipped tires in his spare time and had unusually great beard-grooming tools for living in the forest or being from the 800s AD.

"Can I help you?"

Okay, so he was a Viking lumberjack who never made it all the way through puberty. When he spoke, it seemed like a prank where he moved his lips and a squirrelly thirteen-year-old spoke the words.

"I, err… Are you Michelle's husband?"

The Viking nodded. "And you're the woman who's supposed to have killed her, right?"

Virginia faltered. She hadn't expected him to know who she was. She started to apologize, to turn and leave on the spot, but he stopped her.

"I know you didn't kill my wife. Do you want to come in?"

In answer, Virginia thrust the casserole dish in her hands out to the man. Homemade stuffed shells. Just not homemade by her. For decades, Virginia had occasionally turned up to Luigi's with her own casserole dish, a few folded bills, and the most charming smile she could muster. The proprietor would fill it with pasta and do his best to make it look like it had been baked in that dish instead of plopped in after the fact, then hand the dish to her with a wink.

With a thanks, Michelle's husband took the dish and led Virginia into the house. They passed through a living room, neat and clean and nondescript, and then into the kitchen, where he set the dish on the cooktop and opened a cabinet.

"Something to drink?"

"Do you have sweet tea?"

It was only after he handed her the full glass that Virginia remembered she was here to suss out whether she thought this man might have killed his own wife, and maybe it wasn't the smartest thing in the world to take a drink from him.

He read her hesitation and reached out to take the glass from her hands, taking a sip from it himself. "Not poisoned," he said, handing it back.

Virginia gave a sheepish apology and took a performatively large glug of the drink.

"I know what it's like to have everyone think you're a murderer. Not great, is it?"

Virginia shook her head. Here she was, deep in an investigation with the main goal of proving to everyone that she wasn't a murderer, and she'd gone and made this man feel exactly the way everyone was making her feel.

"I can't decide what's worse. Being seen as a murderer, or knowing that the person I love most in the world is dead and it's my fault."

Virginia's eyes widened. He'd taken a sip of that drink first, right? She hadn't imagined it.

"I didn't kill her," he clarified. "I left work and went to couples therapy like I did every Friday, but Michelle never showed. That was unlike her, but we'd been fighting more and more, and I thought maybe she just needed more time than usual to cool down and wasn't ready to see me yet. When I got home, I found her dead."

"But she wasn't living here, right? She had a room at Breeze Village all the time I've known her."

Her husband shook his head. "We'd make the occasional go at cohabitating again, but it's been probably six months since the real split. Look, I know it doesn't look good, living apart and being in couples therapy and then my wife turning up dead, but I didn't do it."

"Don't worry, I'm the queen of 'it doesn't look good.' No need to explain."

Michelle's husband gave her a small smile, and the two of them stood opposite each other, each leaning against a stretch of counter, just looking at each other. For the first time since Russ died, Virginia felt seen. Understood.

"Sorry, what's your name?" she asked.

"Thomas. Tom, to most people." Tom extended his hand, his giant palm smooth instead of the calloused paw of the lumberjack Virginia expected.

"So if you didn't kill your wife, why is it your fault she's dead? And if she wasn't living here, why was she here that day?"

"It's my fault because I didn't keep my speculating to myself. I got her involved in something she never should have been in. You know Russ, the guy who bought Breeze Village from her?"

Virginia nodded and grimaced. "I'm supposed to have killed him, too."

Tom's eyes widened, and he actually laughed. "That bit of gossip hadn't made it to me. Anyway, the guy seemed off, somehow. I never wanted Michelle to sell the place, period, but definitely not to that guy. I looked him up and couldn't find anything. Absolutely nothing online. And yet here he is with loads of money, ready to buy a senior living center? It was just weird!

"So I told Michelle what I thought, and she dismissed me. Sold the place to him. But lately, she'd been asking me about the research I'd done looking into him. I got the feeling she was finally sensing that something wasn't right with him and starting to look into his past. And then he turns up dead, and then she turns up dead."

"You think she was killed because she was looking into Russ?"

Tom shrugged. "I can't think of any other reason. She had no enemies."

"Can I ask why you were living apart?"

Tom's jaw clenched. He seemed to be considering whether he wanted to answer. Finally, he exhaled and said, "We'd been trying for years to have a kid. Round after round of IVF. Thousands of dollars, gone. And I'd finally had enough. But she wanted to give it one more round, always one more round. It broke us."

"A kid? How old…?" As soon as Virginia realized the words that were falling from her mouth she stopped talking.

Tom gave a low laugh. "Too old to be having kids. But Michelle's younger than she looks. Just over forty but she dresses like she's seventy. I always teased her about it." He looked up and assessed Virginia's outfit. "No offense."

"None taken."

"It's why she sold Breeze Village in the first place, the IVF. In a fight, I'd brought up that even if I was willing to go through the emotional turmoil again, we couldn't afford another round. And she took that to mean that if she came up with the money, I'd be willing to try one more time."

He looked up at the ceiling. Virginia could see he was biting his tongue. His next words came out strangled. "If we'd never had that fight, if I'd never said those words, she wouldn't have sold Breeze Village. She wouldn't have met Russ. She wouldn't be dead."

Tom didn't have any other information for Virginia, and she didn't linger. She apologized for coming and bringing this all up. She wanted to apologize for not even making the pasta herself, but she stopped herself, instead vowing to make a dessert and bring it by some other time. In celebration, maybe, when the killer was caught.

CHAPTER 16

That night, even Stephanie's homemade dumplings couldn't arouse Virginia's appetite. When she turned down a bowl of ice cream after dinner, both kids looked at her with concern.

"What's wrong? Are you sick?" Jack asked.

"I'm not sick. I'm just not very hungry tonight. Really, I'm fine."

But she wasn't fine, and after nearly an hour of tossing in bed, unable to sleep, she made her way to the living room and settled in on the couch for some late-night television. She scanned the channels. NCIS: Los Angeles. House Hunters. The real housewives of someplace. She settled on a cooking competition where chefs were halfway through preparing meat pies and immediately decided Jason was her favorite and Marie should be voted off that week. Who said you had to watch for any real length of time to develop favorites?

"Can't sleep?"

Jack's voice startled her, and Virginia jumped, hand on her chest.

"Sorry."

"It's all right. No, can't sleep. You?"

He shook his head and settled in on the couch beside her. He leaned over to half-snuggle her, and for a moment, it felt like when he and Lucy were children and they'd all snuggle on the couch together for movie nights.

On the screen, Jason made a mistake and burned his pastry crust. Virginia groaned.

"Mom, we've seen this episode like three times. You know he loses this week."

"We have not! And I did not! Way to spoil it for me."

Jack sat up, their brief intimate moment spoiled. "We absolutely have."

"Well, I don't remember having seen it before."

"Isn't that why you're here in the first place?"

Virginia paled at the attack. "What are you trying to say?"

"I'm saying you can't remember anything, and it's maddening!"

Before Virginia could even process the words, Stephanie stomped down the hall and into the living room.

"Can you two shut *up?* I was asleep!"

"I was quiet until Jack here decided my not remembering having seen this episode before merited screaming."

"I don't care who said what at what volume. You both need to cut it out. You're stressing me out constantly!"

"*You're* stressing *me* out constantly!" Virginia said. "Seriously, what is with you lately? The tiniest thing sets you off, and it's getting ridiculous."

"What's with me?" Stephanie balked, then turned to Jack. "You tell her. I'm going back to sleep."

She stalked out of the room, and Virginia turned to Jack. He looked like Stephanie had just told him to walk into battle. All the color had drained from his face, and he looked at his mom more nervous than he'd looked since his SATs.

"Stephanie's pregnant," he finally said.

And all at once, everything made sense. And she felt like a massive jerk.

Virginia couldn't speak. Tears flooded her eyes, and her breathing was shallow. "How long?"

"Nine weeks."

She inhaled a gasp.

"It's been a long road to get here, and she's—we're—terrified of losing it again, so just please be sympathetic and try to keep things as stress-free for Stephanie as possible."

Jack had hardly gotten the words out when Virginia breathed, "Of course. I am so sorry. And so happy for you."

Losing it *again,* he'd said. Virginia's heart broke for them but soared at the thought of a grandchild. She choked on her emotions, and when words weren't possible, she lunged forward and wrapped her son in an embrace. He stiffened, then relaxed and wrapped his arms around her, and they stood that way as the TV judges sent Jason home and pronounced Marie that week's winner.

Sleep came quickly after that, and when Virginia woke the next morning, her swollen eyes stung but her soul felt happy. For a moment, she was disoriented. She reached up and touched her face and tried to remember what had happened, what was wrong. And then she remembered, and the tears fell all over again. She hadn't even left her bed before she was dialing Marney's number.

"I'm going to be a grandma!"

Marney was silent on the other end. Then, "What?"

"Jack and Stephanie."

Marney screamed, and Virginia pulled the phone away from her ear, laughing through her tears.

Over the years, Marney and Virginia had talked grandchildren during many of their beach swims. And after a while, they'd dropped the subject, accepting that it wasn't in the cards for them. Their kids were turning fifty, and though Stephanie was younger, they'd been married so long Virginia had thought she didn't want children.

"I'm going to go by the storage unit to see what I have in the boxes from my old attic. I know there's got to be clothes and toys from when Jack and Lucy were little. I don't know what kind of shape it's in, but there might be something in there they'd appreciate."

"I'll come with you and we can get lunch afterward," Marney suggested.

"It's a date!"

* * *

Virginia and Marney sat for two hours at a table outside the Hickory Hawk, talking through bites of pizza. Virginia felt like she was glowing, joy radiating off her.

"But the pressure's really on to get out of their house and off on my own now."

"What do you think you'll do?"

Virginia took another bite of pizza as she considered it. "As things are now, I think buying a little condo and getting someone to come help with the things I can't do myself is probably my best option. Breeze Village and Harbor Vale are out of the question as long as I'm a reputed killer."

"But you don't want to live alone in a condo."

"I've overstayed my welcome already. It's time to be practical."

Marney raised her eyebrows at Virginia. "Fair enough. But what if you crack the case and put the real killer behind bars? Then you won't be a reputed murderer. You'll be a verified hero. And for the second time!"

Virginia couldn't stop the smile spreading across her face. "I don't think you're supposed to be encouraging me to try to track down a killer."

"Not encouraging! Just speaking in hypotheticals. If you were to go from possible murderer to definite hero, the world would be your oyster. You'd still want to move into Breeze Village, right?"

"Of course! But now, with Russ and Michelle dead, it doesn't seem like a very stable choice. Who's running the place now?"

"Liam thinks it's him," Marney scoffed. "Haley's stepped up a lot. If Cindy's actually looking to sell, I guess it's possible Hashim will take over and we'll become Harbor Vale 2.0."

"I wonder if Michelle's husband would try to buy it. I imagine he'd need to hire someone to run it, though."

Marney froze, pizza slice halfway to her mouth. "Husband?"

Virginia nodded enthusiastically. "Michelle has a husband, and I paid him a visit."

Marney looked equal parts skeptical and excited.

Virginia recounted her visit to Tom, the Viking lumberjack tire-flipping not-murderer.

"He thinks Michelle was killed because she dug up something on Russ's past? Something someone didn't want her to know?"

"That's what he told me," Virginia said. "He's got a point. It is weird how Russ turned up out of nowhere with oodles of money and no traceable background."

"Is it, though? I mean, do either of us have any background someone could look up if we left Seaview? Maybe he just wasn't interested in social media. Maybe he was a private person."

That wasn't what Virginia wanted to hear. She wanted Marney to agree with her wholeheartedly and say something that gave her an idea of what to pursue next in the investigation. But she had to admit Marney had a point.

"What do you think about Cindy?" Virginia asked. "If Michelle really was killed because she found something from Russ's past, it seems like Cindy would be the one to know all his secrets and maybe want them to stay secret."

The corners of Marney's mouth turned down. "I don't

know. Russ was clearly seeing at least a few other women. Maybe Cindy didn't know all his secrets."

Not eager to bring their afternoon to a close, Marney and Virginia headed to the beach to walk on the pier. The sun beat down punishingly, but it was gusty on the beach, and the wind alleviated the heat. The sand was crowded with families and tourists enjoying the summer, and kites dotted the sky. Fishermen lined the side of the pier where they were allowed to cast their lines.

"I've got a bite!"

A familiar voice made Virginia squint down the walkway, and in the line of fishermen, she spotted Hashim from Harbor Vale tugging at his fishing rod, the rod starting to bow with the weight of whatever was at the other end. And next to him was Dick, no walker in sight.

"Give me a hand, will you?"

Dick leaned over and helped brace the rod while Hashim cranked the reel. The rod bowed more and more, and Dick and Hashim reeled and tugged at it. Excited shouts went up around them as they got closer and closer to hauling in the giant fish. Then the line snapped, and both Dick and Hashim toppled over from the sudden release.

Dick cursed as he pulled himself to his feet, then offered Hashim a hand. And to Virginia's surprise, he picked up his own rod, brought it back over his shoulder, then cast it forward in a perfect arc.

"Did you see that?" Virginia asked.

Marney nodded.

Virginia led them back toward their cars, not wanting Dick to see them and know he'd been caught out.

"That bastard," she said once they were standing on asphalt, off the pier and away from the crowds. "He's supposed to be handicapped, takes his walker everywhere he goes, yet here he is with no walker in sight, swinging a fishing rod with perfect ease."

"Are you going to confront him?"

"Eventually," Virginia said. "I want to know what else he's lying about."

THE NEXT DAY, Virginia headed to Breeze Village to have a little chat with Dick. She was halfway there, squinting into the bright afternoon light, when a hulking black SUV pulled up behind her. Its bright lights were on despite it being the middle of the day, and it looked menacing in her rearview mirror. And then it came closer, and closer, and closer, until Virginia thought if she slowed down the slightest bit, the SUV would ram her car from behind.

She changed lanes, hoping the driver was merely impatient to get wherever they were going and would speed off around her. The SUV changed lanes with her, maintaining the near nonexistent distance between them.

Virginia sped up. The SUV matched her speed.

When she was nearly in tears, anxious over being followed, the vehicle finally changed lanes and sped past her. She breathed a sigh of relief. And then the car swerved in front of her and slammed on its brakes.

Virginia screamed and turned the wheel hard, the brakes of her own car protesting as she tried to avoid slamming directly into the monster vehicle. Her car lurched as the tires left the pavement and hit grass and dirt and tree roots. Her head jerked back and forth, and her teeth came down hard on her tongue. She cursed, brake pedal planted all the way on the floor of the car but absolutely no use, and then her car collided with a tree and came to a stop.

CHAPTER 17

The next thing Virginia knew, she was in a hospital bed with an IV attached to her hand and a monitor beeping rhythmically beside her bed. Her eyes fluttered open. The room was dim, and she could make out a few blob-like shapes along the wall. Her eyes fluttered shut again, and the next time they opened, the room was splashed in sunlight.

"Mom, you're awake!" Lucy's voice was the first thing Virginia heard. "She's awake!"

"Virginia." A bony hand covered in soft skin gripped her own, and Virginia looked up to see Marney staring down at her, worry etched across her face.

Lucy dropped down onto Virginia in the closest thing to a hug they could manage with Virginia in the hospital bed. Another figure moved in her peripheral vision, and Virginia turned to find Jack standing there.

"Hi, Mom," he said.

"Hi, sweetie."

A nurse entered the cramped room and chased her

family out before turning to Virginia. The nurse was a tall, slender black man, and he moved with the efficiency of an expert. Virginia continued to drift in and out of consciousness, vaguely aware of pain in her head and all down her body, and didn't resist as the nurse checked her over and cleaned her up.

When Virginia fully came to, her family was back in the room, this time minus Jack but plus Dylan and Lawrence.

"How am I?" she asked. She wanted to be happy to be awake, happy to see all her limbs were intact, happy to have her loved ones close. Instead, she felt anger rise up in her, frustrated that once again she knew the least about her own situation.

"You've got a mild concussion," Lucy said. "And some bruising. Nothing's broken."

Virginia spied several vases of flowers on a table in the corner, a cake, and a single card propped up. "How long have I been here?"

"Since yesterday. Someone called the police after seeing your car, and then an ambulance brought you here straight away yesterday afternoon."

Virginia gestured to the table. "Who are those from? Who knows I'm here?"

"Lawrence and I brought the flowers," Marney said. "We wanted to brighten the space a little. The card is from Colleen, and judging by the looks of it, the cake is from Gemma."

Colleen? Virginia tried to lift up her arm to reach toward the table. Lucy handed her the card, but without her glasses, Virginia couldn't make it out.

"What does it say?" She handed the card to Marney.

"'I hope I'm wrong and you're not in the hospital, but in case I'm correct—and I always am—I hope whatever has you in there subsides soon. Thinking of you. Gemma wanted to send along a treat, but I don't need my visions to know you probably shouldn't eat it.' And then she drew some hearts at the bottom."

More anger flared up in Virginia. Colleen had been nothing but unhelpful since Russ's death, and a card proclaiming she'd had a vision that Virginia was in the hospital only rubbed it in.

"I need you to try to recount for me what happened," Dylan said. Her voice was official, but sympathy lay beneath.

"A big, black SUV ran me off the road."

"Do you know what make or model? And did you get a look at who was driving?"

Virginia shook her head. No and nope. Dylan nodded and tried to conceal her disappointment, but it was evident anyway.

"When did you first see the SUV? How long were you on the road together, and how exactly did they run you off it?"

Virginia described how she'd been halfway to Breeze Village from Jack's house when the vehicle seemed to appear out of nowhere behind her. After following her dangerously close, they'd cut her off and braked, so she'd swerved and hit the tree. The windows were tinted, so she hadn't seen the driver, and if she'd been able to see the license plate or vehicle make or model at the time, she couldn't remember now.

Dylan took some notes, then stood and approached Virginia's bedside, taking her hand and giving it a gentle squeeze. She leaned down and kissed Virginia on the cheek, her dark hair brushing Virginia's face.

"I'm sorry to bring it up," Dylan said quietly. "But we're gonna find whoever did this."

With another squeeze of her hand, Dylan was gone.

"So I've got a concussion, eh?" Virginia asked.

Lucy nodded, her face the very picture of concern and attention.

Marney cracked a smile. "I guess it was your turn, huh? Lawrence, you're next."

Virginia remembered the fear and guilt she'd felt standing next to Marney's own hospital bed in the spring. The fact that Marney could have a sense of humor about it now was a mercy Virginia didn't think she deserved.

"I think it's only the ones who go investigating criminals that wind up here with a concussion," Lawrence said. "Since I'm firmly in the *mind my own business* camp, I should be safe."

When Lucy left and only Marney and Lawrence remained, Virginia said, "I don't know what to do now."

"Drink lots of fluids, avoid caffeine and screens, and rest up," Lawrence said.

"I mean about the investigation."

Marney and Lawrence frowned at her, but neither said anything. They were giving her room to make her own decision, and while Virginia appreciated it, she felt torn. Someone wanted her dead, it seemed, and she could only assume it was because of her digging into Russ's and Michelle's deaths. With a grandchild on the way, her already strong desire to remain alive had another contributing factor, but if someone would run her off the road to stop her investigating, she figured she had to be getting close.

* * *

VIRGINIA WAS under strict instructions to avoid screens and high excitement, so bingo and some time playing wing-woman for Lawrence seemed like the right move. Anything to get her out of the house and out from under her kids' supervision.

"You just point out the guy, and I'll sidle on over to him and talk you up," she said. She grabbed her dot marker and assessed the card in front of her.

"Don't look, but the man two tables back to our right with the white hair. I met him a week or so ago at the bowling alley."

Virginia turned conspicuously in her chair.

"I said don't look!"

"You said, 'don't look' and then told me where he was sitting and what he looks like, which implies 'look.'"

"This was a terrible idea."

Virginia made a *harumph* sound and dabbed sweat from her forehead with a handkerchief. "You're telling me."

It was her first bingo game since the tournament gone wrong, and prior to the tournament, Virginia saw bingo as the old people's game for people who aren't good enough to play rummy or poker. "It's all luck," she'd complain after another loss. And leaving the tournament as a murder suspect hadn't done much to sweeten her on the game.

"Thank you for being here," Lawrence said.

The bingo game was held at the American Legion. Virginia thought it would be more pleasant indoors with air conditioning than in a tent like the tournament Lawrence's bowling team had put on a few weeks ago. She was wrong. The air conditioner was on the fritz and the place smelled like stale beer and fried food after the fish fry they'd held two days prior. Wood paneling covered the walls, and small windows let in a meager amount of light. The space felt claustrophobic, and Virginia looked around to see whether there was punch or cake to take the edge off. Instead, all she saw were bulletin boards featuring political fliers.

"Who's that woman? She looks familiar."

"That's Susie Hoffman. She's running for state Senate."

"Isn't it a little early to be campaigning?"

Lawrence shrugged. "She lost on account of the senior citizen vote last time around, and she's pretty serious about making sure that doesn't happen again."

"Oh, she's the one trying to repeal the laws about retaking the driving test to renew your license?"

"That's the one." Lawrence's focus was on his bingo card. He'd filled in nearly half the squares and was one call away from bingo in three different directions.

From the table behind them a woman piped up, "You talking about Hoffman?"

Lawrence nodded. Virginia turned in her seat to look at the woman. She had bright red hair with an inch of gray roots, flat to the top of her head and then poofing out like a triangle before stopping bluntly at her shoulders.

"Yeah. Do you think you'll vote for her?"

The woman shrugged. "She seems like a weasel. She only cares about us old folk because we crushed her last go around. But at the same time, if someone wants to pander to me, I'll take it."

The woman next to her chimed in, "I don't like her. I heard she started dating some guy who works at a retirement home to get closer to the people she's trying to win over. Weasel-looking fellow himself, actually."

Virginia's brows knit together. Breeze Village and Harbor Vale were the only retirement homes in Seaview.

"That Breeze Village guy, right? I saw him at one of her rallies. I heard there would be Miss B's, and I thought about how I hadn't had Miss B's in a while, so I figured I'd go see what she was all about. And it turned out there wasn't Miss B's at all! It was KFC. I turned around and walked out, but not before I saw that Hoffman and her beau. You're right, Lucille. He is a weasel-looking fellow. Fitting!"

A memory resurfaced. When Virginia had approached Michelle to demand being put back on the Breeze Village waitlist, she'd been arguing with Liam. And Virginia was pretty sure she'd made a jab at him about his politician girlfriend.

"Virginia." Lawrence elbowed her in the side and pointed down at her card, which he'd taken to filling in for her while she was talking with the women behind them. "You got bingo."

"What? Oh, bingo. Bingo!" She stood up and waved her card above her head. "I got bingo!"

When she returned home that evening, Jack and Stephanie were in the living room, reading on separate ends of the couch. Jack was seated upright and straight, and Stephanie lounged with her feet on his lap. At her entrance, both of them turned and looked at her with thinly veiled concern.

"How did it go?" Jack asked.

Virginia held up the stack of bills she'd won, showing off her cash prize. "I'd say it went pretty well."

Stephanie beamed at her, and Virginia crossed the room and thrust her arm out toward her and Jack.

"For you. Enjoy a nice dinner out sometime."

"Oh, we couldn't," Stephanie protested even as Jack accepted the money.

"You've done too much for me. You're still doing too much for me. Let me do this."

She'd been excited to give this gift to them but hadn't realized how important it would feel. She couldn't keep from beaming as she handed it over, the feeling of having something of her own to give making her proud.

When Virginia looked at her phone before crawling into bed, there was a text from Marney waiting. *Sundae party at Breeze Village tomorrow,* along with three ice cream emojis. The unwritten second half of the message being *Dick will be there. Time to see what else he's lying about?*

CHAPTER 18

Nothing got the Breeze Village residents to participate in activities like free food. Miss B's after memorials had the best turnout, but a sundae bar seemed to be a close second. Soft music played in the background, and several tables were filled with board games, card games, and puzzles for the residents to enjoy while they ate their ice cream.

When Dick got up to leave after finishing his sundae, pushing his walker ahead of him as always, Virginia made her move. She followed at a distance, waited until he was in the elevator, then hurried in to join him just before the doors closed.

"What floor?" Dick asked.

"Whichever one you're headed to."

Dick gave her a quizzical look. Virginia returned a steely glare.

"How come you're allowed to live upstairs, anyway, with your walker? I thought in case of a fire emergency, you had to be able to take the stairs."

Dick shrugged. "I'm not too worried about it. There hasn't been a fire here since it opened, and I don't anticipate one any time soon."

Not too worried about it. *Of course, he's not. He's as spry as a spring chicken and would have no trouble on the stairs.*

"I saw you at Harbor Vale the other day."

The elevator doors opened on the third floor and Dick shuffled out, Virginia hot on his heels.

"I have a lot of friends there from my pre-retirement days," Dick said.

"It seemed like you're pretty friendly with the owner, too."

"I've been spending a good deal of time over there and got to know him a bit. To tell you the truth, I'm not so sure I made the right choice coming here. My son was so insistent Breeze Village was the place for me, but now I've hardly been here six weeks and there've already been two murders and a kickbacks scandal. I can't help but hope the rumors are true and Hashim Odeh buys this place and calms things down."

"Your son convinced you to move here?"

Dick pursed his lips and gave a short nod. "Turns out it was more out of concern for his own finances than my wellbeing. He's a doctor. He was one of the ones involved in the scandal."

"He must have been pretty upset with Michelle after her announcement, then."

Dick turned away and quickened his pace toward his room. "I don't want to talk about it."

When they reached his room, Dick pulled the door

open and shuffled inside, stopping just inside the door so Virginia couldn't follow him in. He turned to shut the door on her, but Virginia piped up, "I know your handicap is a lie!"

Dick stood frozen in the doorway for a moment before sticking his head out and looking around the hall to make sure no one was there. Then he gestured for Virginia to come inside and shut the door behind them.

"I saw you fishing with Hashim. No walker in sight. Turns out you can swing a fishing rod just fine."

All the color had left Dick's face.

"You absolutely could have killed Michelle to get revenge on her for shutting down your son's practice."

Shock was replaced by confusion. "What does my handicap status have to do with Michelle? You think I killed her?"

"Michelle was hit over the head. That's how she died."

"Well, I didn't know that." He rounded on her. "How did you know that? That only makes it look more like you did it."

Virginia took a breath and ignored the jab.

"And you're awfully friendly with Hashim, especially saying you want him to buy Breeze Village. I assume you know he tried to before?"

Dick looked at Virginia with suspicion but didn't deny the question.

"Then Russ came into the picture and ripped the rug out from under him. I'm sure that made Hashim mad. And if you're such good friends with him, maybe you decided to take care of Russ for him. Then your friend gets what he wants, and you get what you want: Breeze Village becoming a second Harbor Vale."

"That's ridiculous," Dick sputtered.

"We'll see if the police think it's ridiculous when I tell them everything I know."

"What exactly are you planning to tell them?" Dick's voice shook as he spoke.

Virginia raised her eyebrows. She had him where she wanted him. "Murders aside, I imagine there will be a citation of sorts for faking a disability to secure a handicap placard. I also imagine the residents here will have something to say about it."

If it were possible for Dick's face to pale any further, it did. "Please don't tell them."

"What will you give me in return?"

Dick stared at her, trying to figure out what to offer.

"Information," she said. "You're a liar and a jerk, but I don't think you killed anyone. But if you know anything that can help me figure out who might have, I want to hear it."

The two stared at each other in silence. Virginia waited a beat. Then two. Then dropped her gaze and turned to leave.

"Wait!" Dick called.

Virginia turned, eyebrows raised in question.

"Hashim was at the casino when we were there. When, err, when Russ died."

Virginia had to put a palm on the wall to steady herself.

"I went to try my luck at roulette when I got tired of bingo, and I saw him at one of the card tables."

Virginia clicked her tongue in disgust. "You'd sell out your friend to keep your special parking space?"

"Don't tell him I told you." Dick's face was lowered, shame reddening his cheeks.

Virginia shook her head and left.

CHAPTER 19

Virginia saw herself marching up to Harbor Vale, the automatic doors flying open just before she walked into them, everything in perfect timing. She saw herself maintain a cool and composed expression when she found Hashim in the lobby and told him she needed to speak with him privately. She saw him melting before her and immediately confessing to both murders just before the police rushed in and hauled him off. But that wasn't what happened.

She'd been quicker to tire since her accident, and her leg sometimes throbbed without warning. Leaving Dick's room at Breeze Village, she'd been limping heavily by the time she got down to the parking lot and had to make a detour home to rest, take some Tylenol, and grab the cane she never used if she could help it. This was too important a mission to let her embarrassment over needing a cane stop her.

It was early evening by the time Virginia hobbled

across the Harbor Vale lot, leaning heavily on the gaudy pink cane Jack had bought her. She gripped the foam handle tightly as she approached the sliding glass doors.

Instead of flying open automatically as she approached, the doors remained steadfastly shut in her presence, despite the stickers declaring they were automatic. Virginia stood in front of them, waiting, wondering if she was somehow standing wrong. She took a step back, then another step forward, moved slightly to the left, and then *voila!* The doors slid open.

"Sorry about that," a woman said from behind the main desk. "The doors have been giving everyone trouble lately. We've got a serviceman coming tomorrow to check them out and hopefully fix them."

Virginia cleared her throat and lifted her chin. "I'd like to see Mr. Odeh, please."

The woman faltered. "He's not available at the moment. Do you have an appointment?"

"No, but it's important."

"I'm sorry. I can make an appointment for you if you'd like. Maybe sometime next week?"

Virginia did her best not to let her disappointment show. "That's okay."

"Anything else I can help you with?" The woman's voice was bored. She didn't seem eager to help Virginia with anything except finding the door.

Virginia sagged. She needed to find Hashim. "I'll just pay a friend a visit, then. Jan."

The woman pursed her lips and pulled out a clipboard with a visitor log attached. "Name?"

Virginia gave the woman the information she requested. When she asked for Virginia's relationship to Jan, Virginia said they'd lived in the same neighborhood before Jan moved to Harbor Vale.

"So, 'friend,'" the woman said, noting their relationship on the log.

Virginia wasn't sure if *friend* was the right word for it. They'd been in the same social circle for decades. She didn't dislike Jan. But she wouldn't call up Jan to spend time alone when she needed some company. Not unless there was a piece of gossip she was hoping to get.

"Ma'am?"

Virginia looked up. She'd zoned out, and the woman was looking at her warily, holding out a sticker that said *Visitor* in bold letters. Virginia apologized and took the sticker, pasting it to her chest.

"Can you remind me what room she's in?"

The woman read off the room number, and Virginia shuffled to the elevator. She rode the elevator up a floor, made her way down a long stretch of hallway, then turned and walked the length of a second hallway until she found a stairwell. She took the stairs—a herculean effort—back down to the first floor and looked around. *His office has to be here somewhere.*

Virginia recalled Jack and Stephanie being led away from the lobby to the left when they'd met with Hashim without her. That would take them to the opposite side of the square building from where she was now. With a sigh, she steeled herself and began the rest of the long walk around the building.

She didn't come across any familiar faces as she made

her way toward where she hoped Hashim's office awaited. She hardly came across any faces at all. Every room door was shut fast, and no sound drifted her way from any common areas.

When she finally stood before the door a nameplate indicated was the office she'd been looking for, Virginia's stomach danced nervously. She hadn't really believed she'd find it. Now she worried that maybe Hashim wouldn't be in there, that she wouldn't be able to find him and talk with him. Then she worried that maybe he would be in there and she'd have to talk to him after all. She was trying to decide which outcome was worse when the door swung open and Hashim nearly ran her over leaving his office.

"Whoa, sorry about that." He narrowed his eyes at her. "You look familiar."

"Virginia Walker." She shifted her cane from her right hand to her left so she could hold out her dominant hand to shake. "I need to talk with you."

Hashim dropped her hand after a quick shake. "I'm afraid I'm otherwise occupied, but if you go to the front desk, they'll help you make an appointment for another time."

She couldn't let him leave. She couldn't let this opportunity slip past her.

"I know you're buying Breeze Village," she blurted out. "And I know it's the second time you've tried to buy it."

Hashim faltered for a moment, then plastered on a smile. "That's not privileged information. I'm sure a lot of people know that."

"How convenient that the person who bought it out

from under you the first time died and it went back up for sale. And now your competition, who also happens to be the person who didn't sell it to you the first time, is dead, too."

"What's this about?" Hashim stepped in close and looked around, apparently trying to decide whether to take this conversation into his office.

"You needed Russ out of the picture. You had a grudge against Michelle for selling Breeze Village to him the first time, and you needed her out of the way so she didn't take it from you this time around."

"If you're implying I had anything to do with those murders, all I have to say is that I am cooperating fully with the police. I have no obligation or intention to cooperate with an eighty-year-old murder suspect playing detective in order to meddle in other people's business. Now, if you'll excuse me—"

Stung, Virginia let Hashim get halfway down the hall before she found her voice again. "I also know you were there when Russ was killed."

Hashim turned quick as a whip, horror written across his face.

"At the casino," Virginia clarified. "Do the police know that bit of information?"

"I was there to gamble," Hashim practically whispered, unlocking and opening his office door and gesturing Virginia inside. "And the police haven't questioned me in relation to Russ, so I don't know what they know. But it doesn't matter anyway, as I was nowhere near Russ the entire time, and it's you they think did him in."

Hashim jabbed his finger at Virginia with the word

you. His voice was level, but his breathing was uneven and his eyes were darting around the room. He was scared.

"And Michelle?"

Fire flashed in his eyes at the mention of her name. "I didn't kill her, but I can't say I'm sad to see her go. Yes, I'm buying Breeze Village. But Cindy's been planning to sell it to me and not that bitch all along."

"How can you be sure?"

Hashim deliberated. "I've been seeing her. She never wanted to buy Breeze Village in the first place. Russ wanted it. She wanted to move to the city, but Russ was insistent. Now she's going to sell it to me and get the hell out of Seaview."

Before Virginia could ask any other questions, Hashim crossed the room in two large strides and pulled the door open.

"Next time, make an appointment."

* * *

LAWRENCE SHOWED up at Jack's house the next morning and let himself in while Virginia was eating cereal at the kitchen island. "Knock, knock," he said on his way in instead of knocking.

"To what do I owe the pleasure of this surprise?"

"Word on the street is some of the residents at Breeze Village are having a little party today to celebrate Marney's crochet shop opening. I thought I'd pick you up and we could go together."

You mean you thought I would have missed the memo and

not shown up if you hadn't come and picked me up. Never mind that he was correct.

"A party? Wasn't there just a party at Breeze Village yesterday? The ice cream sundaes."

"That was put on by Breeze Village. This is put on by the residents, and it's to celebrate Marney and her accomplishments."

Virginia felt guilty for her initial reaction of dismissal. "Well, that's a lovely idea."

"Marney doesn't know. It's a surprise. Gemma texted us both last night, but you never responded. Hence, here I am."

"Oh." Virginia picked up her phone and checked it. Sure enough, when she pressed the power button, nothing happened on the screen. "No battery. I must have forgotten to plug it in."

She tried to brush off the frustration. She hadn't forgotten. Her phone was just dead.

"Gemma said they're ordering pizza, and Jane's picking up balloons."

"What should we bring?" Virginia peered out the window at the small garden she'd cultivated in front of the house. Several of the flowers were struggling against the sweltering summer heat, but the marigolds and geraniums were beautiful. She thought she might bring a few small vases of them to put on the tables in the dining room.

"A cake," Lawrence answered. "Gemma said she's making one."

"Oof, then we absolutely need to bring one. Let me see if we have eggs." She stood and started rooting through the fridge and cabinets. "Do you think some little flower arrangements would be nice, too?"

Two hours later, the two pulled into the Breeze Village lot, Lawrence carrying a small box with five little flower arrangements tucked inside, Virginia carrying a sheet cake.

"Oh, good, you're here!" Gemma hurried to the door with her arms outstretched, bat wings flapping as she crossed the floor and wrapped Virginia in a stifling hug. When she pulled back from the hug, she looked down at the cake and frowned. "I made a cake, too. I guess it's nice to have plenty."

The dining hall started to fill up as noon approached. Jane came bearing balloons and tied them to the table where they'd put the pizzas. Lawrence placed Virginia's arrangements on the tables, and finally, Ronald and Patricia came in with their arms laden with pizza.

"Where's Marney?" Virginia asked Gemma.

"Colleen took her to get their nails done. They should be back any minute."

When Marney and Colleen walked through the front doors, a disorderly chorus of "Congratulations" rang out, and Marney turned beet red. She opened her mouth and closed it again three times before finally giving up on saying anything, instead stepping forward to hug Virginia.

"Gemma did all of it," Virginia said.

"You shouldn't have."

"Nonsense." Gemma was in her element, entertaining and making someone she loved feel special. "This is a big accomplishment! You've been crocheting like a fiend, and now you've got your own website up and running! It's huge!"

"I had a lot of help."

Lawrence had found a college student to help Marney set up her online store, but Virginia had tears forming in her eyes with how proud of her friend she was.

"Don't be so humble," she told Marney. "You worked hard for this."

Marney made the rounds, thanking the people who showed up. By popular demand, she retreated to her cottage to fetch a few of her wares to show off.

"I have to figure out how to keep Pancake off of these," she said when she returned, brushing cat fur from a gorgeous deep green blanket.

Virginia was halfway through her second piece of cake —first a sliver of Gemma's, which was dry and tough but a major improvement over where she started, then a slice of her own—when the sound of heels on the floor made her look up. No one at Breeze Village wore heels. The residents were all too wobbly to walk in them, and the staff wore sneakers or clogs with thick, supportive soles. Even Michelle had only ever worn sensible loafers. Virginia looked up and saw Cindy making her way across the floor, not pausing to look at the gathering in front of her.

Cindy walked right up to Russ's office and turned a key in the lock, letting herself in and shutting the door behind her. Virginia couldn't pull her eyes from the door. She wanted to go talk to Cindy and see what she had to say about her involvement with Hashim. But she was there for Marney. She dug her fork into her cake and took another bite, then felt a hand on her shoulder.

"Go." Marney was standing by Virginia's side. She nodded toward the office. "Go talk to her."

Virginia gave Marney a kiss on the cheek before setting down her plate and hurrying across the lobby.

* * *

VIRGINIA STARTED TO KNOCK, then decided that if she did, Cindy would only turn her away. Instead, she tried the door handle, and when it proved unlocked she pushed the door open and entered the office before Cindy could object.

"What are you doing here?" Cindy demanded.

Virginia shut the door behind herself. "I wanted to talk with you."

"You can't just barge in here."

Cindy sounded tired. Virginia felt another stab of guilt for breaking into her home. She saw that Cindy had cardboard boxes out, the first one half-filled with a few books and pictures from Russ's shelves.

"It's one of the less pleasant aspects of losing a spouse," Cindy said, turning back to her work. "You're the one who has to deal with all the shit they leave behind." A dark laugh escaped her throat.

Virginia didn't want to, but she smiled a little. When she'd finally reached a state where she could even consider touching Earl's belongings, she'd cursed him for being such a collector. The stamp and coin albums and the old jazz records held no interest for Virginia and were just taking up space and collecting dust, but getting rid of them had felt a bit like trying to cut out her own heart.

"Why couldn't you have been a minimalist?" she remembered shouting at the ceiling while poring over his collections on the living room floor. Still, she'd gone straight from shouting at the ceiling to crumpling onto the floor in tears, missing her husband so much she thought she might die of it, and Cindy didn't look like she felt anything other than disdain for her late husband.

"Are you going to sell this place to Hashim Odeh?" Virginia asked.

Cindy sighed and stared off into the distance. "I guess so. I wasn't, but now it seems he's my only option."

Virginia's brow creased. "You weren't? He said you've been planning to sell it to him for a while."

Cindy shook her head. "I let him think that. I mean, it's in my best interest to have competing offers, right? But I was going to sell it to Michelle in the end."

"Why?"

"Because I knew why she sold it to Russ in the first place. Michelle loved this place." Cindy looked around and grimaced like she wasn't sure how it was possible. "I know what infertility can do to a person, to a marriage. I don't have any interest in keeping this place, and I wanted her to have it back."

"Hashim says you're seeing each other. Romantically."

Cindy nodded and rolled her eyes. "I was ready to tell him it was over, he'd lost, I was selling to Michelle, and then he pulled out this beautiful pair of earrings and kissed me. So I didn't say anything. And then the next time, it was a necklace, and we did more than kiss. And now I'm ready to exit the retirement home business and finally sell this place to him, but when I do, that'll be the end of the jewelry."

"Unless you keep seeing him," Virginia pointed out.

Cindy scoffed like it was the most absurd idea she'd ever heard.

Virginia felt disgusted.

"So mere weeks—was it even weeks?—after your husband dies, you're locking lips with another man and stringing him along for his gifts. And you're loaded! You could buy yourself jewelry whenever you want!"

"You don't know anything about my relationship with Russ. And it's different when it's a gift. Buying it for myself just feels sad and desperate."

Virginia sat. She didn't want to stay, didn't want to spend any more time in Cindy's presence, but she thought if she kept standing she might fall over she was so angry.

"You're selling this place to Hashim to move on with your life. He wants to buy this place; you want to be rid of it. You have a strong motive to keep him out of prison. If he goes down for Michelle's murder, you have to find a new buyer. What's to stop you from lying to provide him an alibi?"

Cindy reached into her purse and pulled out a hotel key. "You want to corroborate his alibi?" She thrust the hotel key at Virginia. "Doubletree on Simons Street. Check with the staff. They'll confirm we were there that night and that we didn't leave the room for the entirety of our stay. The joys of room service."

Virginia stifled a gag.

"And because I know part of you still thinks I offed my

own husband," Cindy added, "I wasn't anywhere near him that night. I was out with a man named Todd, eating lobster and enjoying a weekend away in Atlanta. Russ never wanted to go to the city. He'd get anxious and panicky any time we went. So when he was out of town, I took advantage of the opportunity."

CHAPTER 20

$\mathcal{V}$irginia left the office in a hurry. She couldn't stand another minute in that tiny room with Cindy. When she rejoined the party, the cake was gone, but Gemma was pouring everyone tequila shots from a flask when she thought the staff wasn't looking. Virginia had accepted one and was holding it up in a *Cheers!* motion when her phone rang. She set her cup down and answered it.

"Mom, where are you?" Jack sounded frantic on the other end.

"I'm at Breeze Village. What's wrong? Is Stephanie okay?"

"She's fine. We're fine. But you need to come home. Someone broke into the house."

Virginia's stomach dropped. She grabbed a chair for support. This was because of her, she knew. Someone had run her off the road, had tried to kill her, presumably to get her to stop investigating. And yet she kept digging, and now it was interfering in her kids' lives, too.

Virginia made it to Jack's house in record time, pedal to the floor throughout the drive. She flew through the door as quickly as an eighty-year-old clutching a cane could. She wrapped Stephanie in a hug first, then went to Jack.

"Thank goodness you're okay!" She squeezed her son tight, only releasing him when a squeak escaped his windpipe. "What happened?"

"We came home from an appointment and found the house like this," Jack said.

Virginia looked around. The place was trashed. Drawers hung from their cabinets, contents spilled on the floor. The couch cushions were strewn across the rug. The kitchen cabinets hung lopsided from their hinges, and plates and glasses were smashed on the tile.

"Is anything missing?" Virginia asked.

Jack shook his head, running his hand up and down his jaw as he paced. "Not that we can tell." He stopped pacing and looked up at Virginia. "They broke into Lucy's, too."

Virginia staggered to the couch. She picked up one of the cushions from the floor and then sat, hanging her head in her hands. Lucy's house was smaller than Jack's. It was part of the reason she'd been staying almost entirely with Jack and Stephanie. That, and it got tiring moving her things between the two houses every two weeks like a kid with divorced parents.

"Same thing, nothing missing?" Virginia asked.

Jack nodded, then picked up a cushion and set it beside Virginia's on the couch, sitting and assuming the same head-in-hands position.

Police arrived moments later to take their statements. Two officers Virginia didn't know knocked at the door, looked around, and asked what happened. Then Dylan arrived in her Subaru instead of a police car.

"I was at home when Officer McNeil gave me a call and said a friend of mine had been robbed. I came as quick as I could."

"I don't think we've been robbed, exactly," Virginia said. "From what Jack can tell, they didn't take anything."

"Except our sense of security," Stephanie said through tears.

Dylan left the police work to her officers, instead comforting and sitting with Virginia and Stephanie on the couch while Jack followed the officers through the house. She swept up as much of the broken ceramic and glass in the kitchen as she could and made coffee. She brought out two mugs—the two most intact, one with a minor chip in the lip and one missing its handle—and gave them to Virginia and Stephanie.

"I think I might need something stronger," Virginia said.

"I'm not supposed to be drinking caffeine," Stephanie said.

"One cup won't hurt," Virginia assured her, and Stephanie downed the mug while Virginia went to see if any of the liquor had survived the burglary.

When Dylan and her officers had left and only Virginia and her kids remained in their ravaged home, Jack turned to Virginia with his hands on his hips.

"This has to stop," he said. "Whatever you're involved in. Your investigation. It was dangerous to you before, but now it's bringing danger into our lives, our home. It can't continue."

Virginia nodded gravely. She knew she had to give up. It felt different when the danger to her family was hypothetical, a vague possibility. Now it was real, and she'd sooner go to jail for a crime she didn't commit than bring more of this chaos on her kids.

"If I find out you're even so much as thinking about investigating on your own anymore, you'll have three days to find someplace else to live."

Virginia nodded again. "Don't worry. I'm done."

Jack nodded, but his eyes were narrowed. He didn't believe her.

Virginia felt a lump forming in her throat. "I'm done," she repeated. Her voice cracked, and she excused herself to her room. At the sight of all her belongings strewn across the carpet, she broke down crying. She felt angry, violated, scared; she wanted to punch whoever had done this. No, she wanted to hit them over the head with her cane. But the police officers didn't seem optimistic that they'd find the culprits, and Virginia couldn't look into it anymore herself. The thought that they'd get away with it kept Virginia awake until the sun started to peak above the horizon, until finally, sheer exhaustion dragged her under.

* * *

VIRGINIA WENT to Marney's the next day. She needed comfort and to get out of the wreck that was the house. She knocked twice but got no answer. Perplexed, she looked down at her watch. It was one in the afternoon. Marney hadn't mentioned any plans. Virginia knocked again, then tried the doorknob. It was unlocked.

Virginia pushed the door open. "Marney?" The only answer she got was the lightning-fast blur of Pancake slipping through the open door and brushing past her legs.

"Shit," she cursed. "Pancake! Get back here!"

The tiny tabby cat streaked across the courtyard, up the stairs, and through the open door where a group of residents were making their way out of the main building and onto the patio.

"Stop that cat!" Virginia hollered, hurrying across the yard.

The residents looked perplexed. Compared to the energetic blaze that was Pancake, they moved like molasses. They bumbled in the doorway as Virginia approached, still shouting for someone to intercept the cat.

"Excuse me!" Virginia shoved past the residents and into the building.

A few astonished faces looked up at her from where they sat in the dining room. No sign of the cat.

"Did you see a cat run through here?" she practically shouted, looking around the room.

Heads shook in unison, and Virginia let out another curse under her breath.

"Heeeeere, kitty, kitty!" she called. "Come out, come out, wherever you are!"

Virginia made it all the way down the hallway and back to the lobby with no sign of the cat. The woman behind the reception desk said she hadn't seen Pancake, the residents in the dining room still said they hadn't seen him, and the Memory Ward was closed off, so he couldn't have run down that hallway.

Tears stung Virginia's eyes. She felt like a walking disaster. Wherever she went, trouble followed for those she loved the most. She didn't know how she was going to tell Marney she'd lost her cat.

She started to turn to go back to the courtyard to look for him there when a crash from Russ's office got her attention. She hurried over and found the door cracked. Pancake was up on top of one of the two filing cabinets Russ hadn't gotten rid of, looking down at her with a playful air about him.

"Get down from there," she commanded uselessly. He'd come down when he was good and ready, she knew. No use trying to tell a cat how to behave.

She looked to see the source of the crash. A paperweight with a big blue wave inside it lay on the floor near the base of the filing cabinet, and Virginia guessed Pancake had knocked it down and that was the noise she'd heard. She leaned over to pick it up, and on her way back to standing, she hit her head on the underside of the large desk that occupied the center of the room. Her hand flew to her head as a few choice expletives tumbled from her lips.

Seeing stars, Virginia took a seat in the oversized leather desk chair. It felt like a powerful seat, like sitting on a huge throne, and Virginia put her hands on the desktop for a moment, enjoying that feeling. On a whim, she started pulling the desk drawers open. This wasn't investigating, she told herself. It was just ordinary, run-of-the-mill snooping. She'd snoop through anyone's desk drawers. And since she wasn't snooping on Russ because he was murdered but just because she could, she figured it couldn't be considered investigating.

The first few drawers were empty, already cleared out by Cindy. Cindy had left a few cardboard boxes behind, half-filled with picture frames, office supplies, and books. None of it looked interesting. When she got to the drawers that hadn't yet been emptied, the contents were disappointing. Manila folders of documents, none of which looked incriminating upon first glance; pens and highlighters and sticky notes; stationary that said *Breeze Village* across the top.

In the bottommost drawer, just as Virginia tired of flipping through uninteresting papers, her fingers touched on something thicker. She pulled it from the desk. It was a picture frame with a photo of a group of coworkers standing outside an office building. Potted plants framed the door, and in the background, mountains rolled against a bright blue sky. The picture had been signed by most of the people within, and in the top right corner, someone had written *Blink Financial, 2018.*

Virginia studied the faces. In the middle of the photo, front and center, was Russ. He was unmistakable. There was no signature next to his face, presumably since it was his own photograph. But when she looked at the other faces, she noticed one that looked familiar in the back right. He looked different with facial hair, but she knew him. It was Liam. But his signature said Jimmy Brandt.

Virginia wiggled the mouse on the desk, but the

computer was off. She pulled out her phone, settling for the small screen and even more frustratingly small keyboard, and typed in the company name Blink Financial. All the top search results were news articles about the company going under, the partners all being arrested for fraud save for one who was believed to have died in a fire after his house exploded. Part of his finger and a few teeth were found in the rubble, but those were the only identifiable remains. His assistant, Jimmy Brandt, went missing shortly thereafter. The partner who died in the fire was named Blake Snyder, and the article included his photo. It was Russ.

* * *

THE ARTICLE DISAPPEARED, replaced by an incoming call taking up the entire screen. It was Marney, and Virginia answered right away.

"Marney, you're never going to believe this," she said.

"Virginia, I need your help." Marney sounded distressed. Virginia thought she might be crying.

"What's wrong?"

"I'm having a panic attack and I can't make it stop. Lawrence can't come help me because he's out with the new girl he's seeing."

Girl? Something was wrong.

"Marney, what's the matter?" Virginia had an ominous feeling in her gut.

"Just please come as soon as you can." Marney gave an address across town, not far from the industrial park where they'd confronted Matt in the spring, where

Marney had wound up on the concrete with a concussion. Then she hung up.

Virginia spun in a circle, needing to take action but not knowing where to start. Pancake was still up on top of the filing cabinet, blissfully unaware that his owner was in some kind of trouble and trying to signal it over the phone—either that or Lawrence had hit a new level of desperation in his search for a partner.

Collecting herself, Virginia hurried from the room. Getting to Marney was the most important thing. She nearly trampled Ronald in the lobby.

"Oh, good, it's you!" she said. "Pancake is up on the filing cabinet in that office. Can you get him down and return him to Marney's cottage? The door's unlocked."

Before he could object, Virginia was gone.

She paused on the top stair in her rush to the parking lot. Two stops over was a huge, black SUV she'd seen before, but never at Breeze Village. Her heart seemed to stop, and for a moment, she felt she couldn't breathe. It was the car that had run her off the road.

Climbing into the back of the vehicle was Liam, and Virginia could see his girlfriend beside him, recognizable from her campaign fliers.

"Liam!" Virginia shouted.

Liam started to turn toward her, then averted his eyes.

"Jimmy!"

This time Liam turned fully, shock covering his already-pale face. His eyes were wide, and she saw him signal to the driver before pulling his door closed. And just like that, the SUV was off, pulling out of Breeze Village.

irginia wanted to follow them, but she knew she had to get to Marney. From the driver's seat, she called Dylan, cursing with every ring until she picked up.

"Dylan!" she shouted. "Marney's in trouble. Fifty-six Clairmont."

"What?" Dylan pulled the receiver from her mouth and Virginia could hear her calling an officer over to give him instructions.

"She called me and said something about Lawrence having a girlfriend. Something's going on that she couldn't say over the phone."

Virginia heard Dylan shouting some orders before she came back on the line. "Virginia, under no circumstances are you to go there alone. I've got officers heading there now."

Virginia hung up the phone and kept driving. Clairmont was on the south side of town. It would take the police ten minutes longer to get there if they were coming from the station. What if Marney didn't have ten extra minutes?

On the drive over, Virginia considered the possibilities. Marney could be confused. Virginia wasn't sure what a panic attack felt like, but she thought Marney might have just been in such a state she misspoke. Unlikely, but possible. Or Marney could be being held at gunpoint, forced to draw Virginia in so whoever wanted her dead—someone working for Liam-slash-Jimmy?—could finish the job.

She considered what she had on her that could be used to defend herself. She had her cane in the back seat. And her purse was getting heavy. She'd been meaning to clean it out, but that just meant it was all the better for whacking a bad guy in the head. And the police were on their way, she reminded herself. Only ten minutes behind her. All she had to do was cause a distraction to keep Marney safe until they arrived.

Virginia pulled into the lot at 56 Clairmont. No other cars were around. She drove around to the back of the building, where there was a big, black SUV parked with the back doors open. It looked identical to the one she'd seen Liam climbing into, but Liam wasn't there. Instead, the second-beefiest man she'd ever seen, narrowly beaten out by Michelle's husband Tom, stood next to the vehicle. He had his gun trained on the back seat, and as Virginia pulled up, he aimed it at her car instead.

"Get out of the car," he shouted when she got close.

She pulled up abreast of the SUV, and in the back seat, she saw Marney sitting with her hands behind her back and a pillowcase over her head. A sob escaped Virginia's throat at the sight, and she instinctively lunged toward Marney.

"I don't think so," the man said.

Virginia looked up at him. The barrel of his gun was pointed at her head, and she realized with a shock that it looked familiar. It was Earl's.

After a string of robberies in the neighborhood when Virginia was pregnant with Jack, Earl went out and bought a gun in the name of self-defense. He went to a shooting range and learned how to use it, and for years, he kept it in his nightstand. When he died, Virginia hadn't wanted to touch it for fear that she'd accidentally shoot herself in the foot. She'd put it in the small safe where she kept the few belongings of his that were valuable or, in the case of the gun, dangerous. Virginia's blood ran cold as she realized it must have been taken when the house had been broken into. She hadn't thought to check the safe. She kicked herself for making the passcode 0-0-0-0.

"Turn around," the man commanded Virginia.

She did as she was told. Her stomach felt leaden. She considered why they would want Earl's gun, and the only reason she could think of was to make it look like Virginia had shot whoever this man was going to shoot. And it looked like that was going to be Marney and herself.

The man tied Virginia's wrists together behind her back, then spun her back around to face him. In a moment of blind fury, she brought her knee up as hard as she could, catching him off guard and colliding with his crotch.

He cried out in pain, and Virginia lurched toward

Marney again, wondering if she was conscious, if she could get out of the car and run if Virginia was able to get the pillowcase off her head.

Before she reached Marney, the man was upon her once again. He grabbed the back of her shirt, tugging her toward him, and threw a pillowcase over her own head. "Fucking bitch," he spat before walking her around the SUV and shoving her into the back seat beside Marney.

Blind, Virginia heard the man shut both back doors, then climb into the driver's seat and start the engine. The car lurched forward and turned out of the parking lot, Virginia and Marney falling over each other in the back seat with their hands bound and no seatbelts keeping them upright. With a sinking feeling, Virginia realized she'd just gotten them taken from the spot where the police would be looking for them. In a matter of moments, officers would be on the scene, but they'd be long gone and no one would know where they were.

* * *

Virginia was hysterical. Tears rolled down her face, soaking the pillowcase that blinded her and causing the scratchy fabric to stick to her cheeks.

"I'm so sorry," she wailed. "I'm sorry, Marney. I got us killed."

Marney was silent next to her, and Virginia wondered whether she'd been drugged, hoping like hell she was still alive and okay.

"I might as well have shot us both myself with Earl's gun. That's what he's going to make it look like, anyway."

She turned her face toward the driver. "Isn't that right? That's what you're going to do, isn't it? Kill us both and make it look like a murder-suicide?"

Sobs racked her frame, and with every turn, her head hit either the window to her left or Marney's shoulder to her right. They'd been driving for several minutes before she thought to count the turns to try to figure out where they were heading. The realization that she'd let them down yet again shook her and reignited her crying.

What might have been five minutes or an hour later, the car came to a stop and the engine cut out. Virginia heard the driver's door open and shut again, followed by her own door opening. Someone pulled her roughly from the car, then walked her around to the other side, where they did the same to Marney. They walked along what felt like a concrete walkway.

"Step up," the muscle man's voice commanded.

They took the step up. A key turned in a lock, and then a door creaked open.

"Watch your step," the man barked as he led them across the threshold, never mind that the only thing they could watch through the pillowcases were vague shadows.

Once inside, the man shut the door behind them and tugged the sacks from Virginia's and Marney's heads. The two women looked around frantically, trying to figure out where they were. Immediately, Virginia realized the space was familiar. Thick, blue carpet. Multicolored cabinets.

"Oh, this is that condo we looked at!" Marney exclaimed. It was the first Virginia had heard her speak since the phone call, and part of her wanted to cry more with relief even though they were likely minutes away from death.

"Remember, that one Stephanie picked out? What is it, Findowrie Street?"

"Shut up," the man snarled.

"It was definitely Findowrie Street, I remember that now. I thought it seemed like the funniest street name, and in all my decades here in Seaview, I'd never heard of the street until we visited this condo. It's such a cute little building. The yellow siding really stands out from the road, doesn't it?"

Virginia wondered if Marney had lost her mind. Part of her wanted to agree with the man, to tell her to shut up. Here they were, moments from being slaughtered, and Marney was remarking on what a cute house it was that they were going to be murdered in.

"Who do you work for?" Marney asked, turning to the man. He looked surprised to have this question levied at him. Marney turned to Virginia. "Do you know?"

Virginia couldn't open her mouth to answer. She'd moved from hysteria to a near-catatonic state.

"Is it the same gang Matt Beaumont ran with? Do you know Matt Beaumont? You know, he pulled a gun on me a few months ago, so this isn't the first time I've had a gun aimed at me. Well, I guess he was actually aiming it at Virginia, but I was behind her and it felt a bit like it was aimed at me. Of course, that time, I got so scared I fainted and smacked my head on the sidewalk. I got a concussion. So I guess this is the first time I've had a gun aimed at me and remained conscious."

The man was looking at Marney like she was speaking in tongues.

"You know what I haven't done? I haven't shot a gun. Eighty-three years old and haven't shot a gun. It seems like you're going to kill us and all, but it would be mighty nice if you'd let me just try out the gun first."

Now Virginia joined the man in looking at Marney like she was speaking in tongues.

"I also don't think I ever had a banana split. If I have, I've forgotten it. And I've never gotten my shoes shined at one of those things that's like a chair up on little wooden bleachers. You know what I'm talking about? Like in the airports?

"Oh, and I've never worn blue lipstick. I've always wanted to try blue lipstick but thought it would make me look dead. I saw a girl downtown the other day wearing blue lipstick and she looked great, but it's different when you're eighty-three. Any little thing and people think you're dead."

"Shut up!" Virginia couldn't stop herself from yelling. "He's going to shoot us, Marney! He's going to shoot you, and then he's going to shoot me, and then he's going to make it look like I shot us both. The gun is Earl's. They stole it from Jack's house, and now Mister Muscle is going to shoot us with it, and everyone is going to think I did it."

Marney's expression softened. Instead of fear, sadness shone in her eyes. "No one would believe you shot me, Virginia."

"You wanna bet?" the man said.

Both Virginia and Marney turned to look at him. He

had the gun raised in front of him and pointed it at Marney's chest.

The world seemed to stop. Ringing filled Virginia's ears. She couldn't tear her gaze from Marney's face, staring down the barrel of a gun. Marney seemed to steel herself, jaw clenched, and only hate showed on her face as she lifted her chin and glared at the man threatening her life.

The man curled his finger over the trigger and pulled. A shot erupted at the same moment Virginia screamed. Behind her, a second crash rang out as the wooden door splintered, kicked off its hinges. Shouts joined Virginia's as officers swarmed the room, rushing first to the man who was already on the ground.

Virginia's head spun as she tried to make sense of what had happened.

"Are you okay?" An officer approached her and put a hand on each of her shoulders, looking into her face and then assessing the rest of her body for injuries.

"Marney," was all Virginia could choke out.

The officer clipped the bindings on her wrists. Across the small space, Virginia saw another officer doing the same for Marney. Marney, who was still standing. Marney, who wasn't lying on the floor in a pool of blood.

She turned to where the man had been standing and found him lying on the floor, clutching his hand to his chest. Blood covered his hands and clothes, and his face was contorted in pain. Two officers kneeled over him.

A hand pressed against Virginia's back and guided her toward the door and out onto the small front lawn. She turned to see Dylan leading Marney out behind them.

"How?" Virginia croaked out.

"Marney's quick thinking," Dylan said. Pride mixed with terror in her voice. "She managed to call the police from the car. From her description, we were able to find the place in time."

"You were stalling?" Virginia asked, turning to Marney in awe.

Marney nodded. "I'm just lucky my phone was in my back pocket. If I hadn't been able to get to it, or if our stellar hitman had thought to take it from me after having me call you... Well, I don't want to think about that."

Virginia grabbed Marney and hugged her tight. "Thank you," she breathed. "Thank you."

Sirens sounded and grew louder until an ambulance pulled up in front of the house. A stream of EMTs and officers filed in and out of the house until eventually a small team rolled the captor out on a cart. Virginia could see that his right hand and much of his arm was blown apart, hardly recognizable.

"We got lucky," Dylan said. "The gun malfunctioned. If it had fired like normal, we'd be in a very different situation right now."

Virginia looked over at Marney. Even with her genius, she'd almost been killed. She'd be dead now if not for a fluke accident.

"He's not talking," Dylan said, looking at Virginia. "Not that he's in any condition to be thinking clearly. Do you know who he's working for?"

Virginia nodded. "I think so."

Susie Hoffman was holding a fundraising event that evening downtown, and Virginia suspected that's where she and Liam had taken off to. By the time Dylan reluctantly agreed to let Virginia and Marney go on the condition that they waited until officers were in place before speaking to Liam, the sun was setting and the event was in full swing.

Hoffman—or her campaign team—had reserved a ballroom in the swankiest hotel in Seaview and organized a dinner with a lineup of speakers and entertainment. In the lobby, Virginia looked over the program a suit-clad attendant handed her. Two local bands were going to play, and a local author, actress, and celebrity chef would speak and share their stories. Finally, a few current members of the state Senate would speak on Hoffman and why they endorsed her to join their ranks.

"The event is semi-formal," the attendant said, looking Virginia and Marney up and down. Both of them had makeup smeared halfway down their faces and their clothes and hair looked like, well, like they'd been kidnapped and held at gunpoint with bags over their heads.

"They're with us," Dylan said. She flashed her badge as she approached, four uniformed officers flanking her.

The attendant held his hands up in front of him and vacated the area.

Dylan waited until she had confirmation via her radio that officers were surrounding the building. She gave Virginia a nod, and Virginia squeezed Marney's hand before pulling open the ballroom doors and walking straight up to where Susie and Liam were standing on a small stage.

Susie's eyes widened, then she immediately composed her face into a picture of serenity. Liam wasn't so skilled at disguising his feelings. His pale face became even more ghastly, and his hands began to tremble at his side.

"Surprised to see us?" Virginia flashed them her best smile, relishing in their looks of horror.

"I'm afraid your muscle man is indisposed," Marney said. "Next time, make sure your hired muscle properly maintains their firearms. Or don't." She shrugged. "This one worked out pretty well for us."

Virginia beamed at her friend, then turned to look Liam square in the face. His eyes darted around, looking anywhere but at Virginia. She could hear the murmuring in the audience, feel the restlessness stirring the room.

"Liam," she said, "or should I call you Jimmy?"

Liam looked like he was going to throw up.

"That's why you had to kill Michelle, isn't it? Or have some muscle man take care of the job? She started digging around into Russ's past, and she figured out that you two aren't who you said you were."

Susie shouted for security to remove them, but no one moved. Everyone was watching in rapt attention, waiting to see how this played out.

"What I don't get," Virginia continued, "is why you killed Russ in the first place."

Part of Virginia feared that Liam hadn't actually killed Russ. She was confident he'd had Michelle killed, since he'd tried to have Virginia killed, too, but she was afraid he'd say he just copied Russ's killer in pinning Michelle's murder on Virginia.

"I gave up everything for that man," Liam said.

Susie turned to him, shocked. "Stop talking," she hissed.

Liam didn't listen. "I changed my name. I gave up my house, my car, my girlfriend. I gave up my entire *life*. He was the one about to go to prison for fraud. I could have stayed in California. But he promised me I'd be his right-hand man, that he'd make us both rich.

"And then I heard him on the phone calling me a neutered lapdog. He gave his wife the VP position in his company and made me the lousy Wellness Director at a stupid retirement home.

"I'd picked up your nail file in the dining room and was going to return it to you, but then I heard his voice and laughter coming from his room, and that's when I heard him on the phone. I didn't plan to… I didn't mean to…"

Liam trailed off, fully shaking now. Virginia almost felt bad for him. Then she remembered being run off the road, remembered her kids' faces when Liam's hired men had broken into their homes.

"And Michelle?" Virginia prompted.

Liam tried to shrug, but it looked more like a seizure. "It's like you said. She knew too much, and she was threatening to go public with the information. With that stupid investigation she started into the kickbacks, she'd already brought so much chaos and scrutiny on Breeze Village.

"I offered her money not to talk, but her price kept going up. I knew she had to go, and you were already a murder suspect, so I figured pinning it on you was the best way to avoid scrutiny. I didn't kill her." He held his hands up as if not offing her himself made it any better. "One of Susie's drivers did."

"Just like one of her drivers ran me off the road?"

Liam nodded. "You should have just stopped asking questions!"

"That was a lovely speech," Dylan said, stepping forward from where she'd been standing in the back of the ballroom. Her officers followed her, then climbed the stairs onto the stage and grabbed Liam and Susie. "You're going to get to tell it again when we get to the station. And again for a judge. You'll probably want to tell it to a lawyer in the meantime."

Liam and Susie went willingly, and the noise level in the room grew as the crowd began to talk amongst themselves.

A teenager in baggy clothes holding a guitar walked up to where Virginia stood with Marney and Dylan. "Uh, my band is supposed to go on next," he said.

Dylan gestured to the stage. "All yours, my friend."

"Cool."

The teenager took the stage, followed by two other kids, and music filled the room. Forks and knives clinked on plates as people resumed eating their dinners. Virginia couldn't help but feel mildly let down that this apprehension didn't come with a round of applause like the last.

"We had a deal," Dylan said, looking from Virginia to Marney. "And now you're going to let me take you to the hospital for a full assessment."

Virginia nodded and took Marney's hand as they followed Dylan out of the room and into her Subaru.

"I don't need a lawyer anymore, do I?" Virginia asked from the back seat.

Dylan laughed. "Not unless you're going to pull anything stupid in the future. But for Russ and Michelle? Nope, I think you're pretty well in the clear. Instead of a lawyer, you'll probably want a PR agent. The *Seaview Gazette* will be breaking down your door tomorrow, I'd guess."

CHAPTER 23

No one from the *Seaview Gazette* broke down her door, but Virginia did receive several requests for interviews and was delighted to find the town of Seaview no longer looked at her with suspicion. Two days later, when she had a knock at her door, she was surprised to find Colleen there holding a plate of cookies.

"From Gemma," she said. "But they're actually all right."

When the two were settled at the kitchen island, red plastic cups of milk in front of them until Jack and Stephanie bought new glassware, Colleen looked at Virginia and sighed.

"I have to apologize."

"For what?"

"I know you wanted my help with this investigation. If I wasn't trying to separate myself from my visions, I might have seen that you were in danger."

Virginia frowned. "You don't owe anyone the use of

your gift."

"But I do," Colleen insisted. "I was given this gift to use it. And lately, I've been hiding from it."

Virginia took another cookie from the plate. Colleen was right. They weren't bad.

"You remember Genie?" Colleen asked.

Virginia nodded. As if she could forget.

"She sold, err, herbal supplements around Breeze Village. I guess she got them from Matt, and some of us took them for chronic pain. And some of us took them recreationally." She gave a mischievous smile. "When she died, I thought maybe I'd try growing some in the garden myself. Then Gemma moved in and loved the idea.

"Then Russ and Liam showed up and I started having these horrible visions. But they weren't like my usual visions. There was no clarity. I couldn't ever make out what was happening. It was just these overwhelming rushes of bad energy and flashes of blood. I wanted to make them stop, so I drowned them out."

Virginia's mouth hung open in shock. "You've been growing drugs at Breeze Village?"

Colleen looked half ashamed. "Michelle caught us, but we paid her off. No one else has noticed." She shrugged.

"I stand by what I said, that you don't owe anyone your visions."

"Well, since Liam's been behind bars, I've felt back to normal. And I'm delighted to say I saw you moving into the room below mine. It was still summertime, so I'd say we'll be neighbors in short order."

Virginia's heart leapt. It was still unclear what the future held for Breeze Village in terms of ownership and what that would mean for Virginia's search for a place to live. She was relieved that her reputation as a murderer was replaced by her reputation as a hero once again. She figured that if Breeze Village was out of the question, she'd probably be allowed into Harbor Vale now.

"What did you see?" Virginia asked. Colleen was never wrong, but she wasn't always right in the way one might expect. If Colleen had just seen her carrying in boxes, she worried that maybe she was helping someone else move into the room instead.

"Your kids were visiting you. And by the way, congratulations, soon-to-be-grandmother."

Virginia's smile glowed, and she reached over and kissed Colleen on the cheek. "Thank you," she whispered.

"I DID NOT THINK this day would come." Jack raised a glass of champagne, and the rest of the room followed.

"Hallelujah!" Stephanie joked, raising her glass of sparkling grape juice.

Laughter erupted. Lawrence and Marney had come to celebrate Virginia's last night before moving into Breeze Village. Lucy was holding Pancake and cooing over him.

"He seems fond of adventures," Marney said. "He's taken to crying every time I leave, so I don't know what to do but bring him along."

Pancake was decked out in a blue bedazzled harness, his leash hanging by the front door. Jack gave a look like he was glad Marney wouldn't have another occasion to bring Pancake into his house any time soon.

The day after Liam's arrest, Cindy and Hashim had finalized the sale of Breeze Village. It was the talk of the town, at least in the senior citizens' circles, much to Virginia's dismay.

"They couldn't have let me be the big news for a few more days?" she'd lamented.

Instead of rebranding, Hashim had decided to keep the Breeze Village name and promote staff from within as much as possible to maintain the charm that made it such a special place. Haley had taken on new responsibility, and while there was an influx of new staff, it felt like the Breeze Village she knew and loved whenever Virginia visited her friends there. Hashim was looking to hire a new General Manager, as right now he was working overtime trying to manage both homes. Still, Virginia trusted him a surprising amount considering not too long ago she'd have bet her life savings that he was a cold-blooded killer.

Virginia piled her plate with lasagna. She'd insisted on cooking dinner for the family on her last night in this house, but then time had gotten away from her and she'd made a hasty trip to Luigi's with a casserole dish in tow.

Boxes lined one wall in the living room. Given how many of her belongings were in storage, Virginia had been surprised at how much she had here to pack up and take with her. Marney had volunteered Dylan to help with the move the next morning, and Virginia was prepared for her role as supervisor while the kids did all the heavy lifting.

"To the best friends and the best kids a woman could

hope for," Virginia said, thrusting her own glass into the air and sloshing champagne on herself.

"To the end of your career as a detective," Lucy said.

"And to my house not being the one that gets ransacked the next time you decide to come out of retirement," Jack added.

"Oh, and to my unborn grandchild," Virginia said, "whose village couldn't be more excited to welcome them."

"Her," Stephanie said quietly.

The entire room turned to look at her. Jack was smiling at her knowingly. The rest of the family was picking their jaws up off the floor and biting back tears.

"To my granddaughter!" Virginia choked out.

Her family raised their glasses in cheers.

The moment was interrupted by a crash from the kitchen that had Virginia throwing her hand to her heart. There, on the kitchen island, Pancake was looking incredibly proud of himself as he peeked over the edge at the shattered glass he'd just knocked to the floor.

"That was brand new!" Jack cried, racing over the toss the cat onto the floor. "Marney, your cat just broke a brand new glass!"

"It's practice for parenthood," she said, scooping Pancake up and rubbing his head.

Virginia couldn't sleep that night, but for the first time in a long time, it was out of excitement, not fear or frustration. After months of waiting and being told no, she was finally moving into Breeze Village. And, she told herself, she was hanging up her hat as a detective. Too much stress. Unless it's a really juicy case, she thought. Or if she was a suspect again. Or if someone asked her to look into something for them. Or if the police were taking too long.

Well, it was a good thing Breeze Village had a reputation for being so calm and quiet. Nothing to tempt her out of retirement there. No siree.

ACKNOWLEDGMENTS

In some ways, writing a second book is easier than a first. In other ways, it's harder. But with the support and love of my friends, family, and readers, writing this, my second book, was a joyful endeavor. Without my support system, this book may never have come to be, and the process of bringing it into the world would certainly not have been what it was. So thank you.

Thank you to Shirali, Jen, Victoria, Leselle, and every other friend who told me I should write a second book, who encouraged me to be proud of what I'd done and to keep going.

Thank you to Tracy Mooring Liebchen, my editor. You asked me to make some changes I did not want to make. This book is undeniably better for it.

Thank you to my family, Mom and Papa and Andrew and Carlee, for talking about Pension for Murder at Christmas and sharing your favorite moments with me. To hear my own book talked about in that way - to hear you sharing your theories and your reactions to the twists I'd dreamed up - was nothing short of magical. You are nothing short of magical. I am lucky to have you.

Thank you to Ken for reading my first book in a day - your day off! - and telling me it was good. Thank you for every single day you asked "Are you working on your book?" and offered me words of encouragement. Thank you for occupying Theo when he has antsies in his pantsies and is making it hard for me to focus. Thank you for tolerating my early alarms for morning writing sprints. Thank you for your genuine support every step of the way. Your love and partnership is the best thing in my life.

And finally, thank you to every single person who read Pension for Murder. Thank you to those of you who left reviews. Your words were such a boost every time I felt like my brain would never churn out another decent idea.

ABOUT THE AUTHOR

A Georgia peach, Kate Maclean grew up in historic Savannah and spent much of her childhood reading Nancy Drew and Hercule Poirot mysteries on her backyard swing.

This lifelong lover of mysteries and crime dramas now lives outside Washington, D.C., with her partner and their cat.

* 9 7 9 8 9 8 5 2 5 0 0 1 5 *